A DARKER MAGIC

There was a table on the stage. The magician asked Freddie to lie down on it and shut his eyes. He covered Freddie's face with a cloth and asked him if he was afraid. Freddie nodded no. The magician turned to the audience and produced a knife with a long curved blade and encrusted with gems. He whispered something to Freddie. Then there was a quick downward thrust of his arm, a gasp from the crowd, and a thud as the blade buried itself in the table.

Someone screamed. A couple of the younger ones started wailing for their mothers.

The magician picked up the cloth and carried it to the far end of the table by Freddie's feet. Setting it down gently, he turned to smile at the audience, and with a flick of his hand snatched away the cloth. There was Freddie's head . . . and it spoke.

A Darker Magic

MICHAEL BEDARD

AN AVON FLARE BOOK

AVON BOOKS
A division of
The Hearst Corporation
105 Madison Avenue
New York, New York 10016

Copyright © 1987 by Michael Bedard
Published by arrangement with Atheneum/Macmillan Publishing
Company
Library of Congress Catalog Card Number: 86-28829
ISBN: 0-380-70611-3
RL: 6.2

First Avon Flare Printing: August 1989

K-R 10 9 8 7 6 5 4 3 2

For Martha

Presentiment—is that long shadow—on the lawn—
Indicative that suns go down—
The notice to the startled grass
That Darkness—is about to pass—

Emily Dickinson

Chapter 1

The house was far too small for two adults, three children, and a monster. The monster was outside her bedroom door now, repeatedly slamming his toy truck against the wall, and making noises to simulate the roar of the motor and the squeal of brakes.

Emily Endicott sat in her basement room, half awake, watching about a week's worth of patience drain away onto the braided rug. The next time Albert slammed his truck into the wall she was going to open the door and wring his sweet little neck.

She cupped her hands over her ears and hummed to cut the noise. When you lived in a bungalow with a small army, you sought peace in strange ways. Take mother, for instance, who wore cotton balls in her ears and held extended conversations with the kitchen appliances.

The humming helped, except it was difficult to think and carry a tune at the same time. Her diary stared up hopefully at her from the desk.

The desk was not really a desk. Actually it was a kitchen table that had refused to keep up with the family. It had given up when Charles had abandoned his high chair, and had been deposed to the basement room. There it had languished in a corner,

1

propped against the wall, legs amputated and bundled together with sticky tape beside it.

Back then the room had been called "the junk room." It did its best to live up to its name. People more or less just opened the door, pitched whatever it was in, and prayed. It was not a room you showed to company.

Mind you, most company couldn't manage the basement in the first place. It had what you might call a low ceiling. If you were more than five-foot-five you needed either a rubber neck or a good chiropractor. The ceiling was done in a strikingly modern design of cobwebbed beams, sweaty pipes, and frayed wiring, illuminated at intervals by bare bulbs on pull chains. Mr. Endicott, five-foot-eight, regularly walked into one of the bulbs on the way to his workbench. A supply of fresh bulbs was kept in the cold room. The floor beneath the basement stairs was thick with dust and the broken shells of bulbs.

Emily heard a dull thud over the humming as the truck slammed into the wall again, followed by a squeal of brakes. Albert had yet to learn that the brakes were to be applied *before* the crash. There was a good chance he might not live long enough to learn.

In the months immediately following Albert's birth Emily had caught herself going quietly insane. She was still upstairs then, in the back bedroom. For the first six months, mother and dad had kept the crib with them at night, beside the studio couch they slept on in the living room. Then one night the crib managed to snake its way down the hall and into her bedroom. It had been there ever since. She hadn't.

It had taken about a month of working her existence around the baby's schedule before elaborate fantasies of infanticide burst full-blown into her brain. Shortly before they threatened to slop over into what her mother liked to call the "real world," Emily decided to clear out the basement room.

Mother had come downstairs to put a load in the machine while she was in the midst of it. "And just what do you think you're doing, young lady?" Hands on hips.

"Moving."

Mother laughed.

Upstairs, Albert was screaming to be fed. Any normal kid would have had a bottle stuck in its mouth. Not Albert. You stuck a bottle in Albert's mouth and he looked at you like you were crazy. You could even hold him real close and stick the nipple through the buttonhole of your sweater, and he still wouldn't buy it. No, Albert knew what he wanted, all right. And right now she was standing at the foot of the stairs feeding underwear to the washing machine.

"What are you talking about?" her mother had asked.

"It's really pretty simple, mom. I'm moving out of that zoo we call my room upstairs and coming down to live with the centipedes."

There were centipedes, too. Three inchers. Well, maybe two, but they looked about a foot long when one of them decided to take a little stroll while you were down there. If she saw one now she hoped she wouldn't scream.

"Well, we'll just see what your father has to say about this."

"Fine. In the meantime do you think you could give me a hand getting the bed down the stairs?"

Actually, once it was done, everyone thought it was a great idea. In about a year's time it would work its way around to being *their* idea, which was always the way. That didn't matter, though. All that really mattered was that at last she had someplace where she could just go and close the door behind her.

She squeezed her eyes shut now and tried to summon up the dream she'd been awakened from by Albert's banging. For the past couple of weeks, since school had ended, she'd been having incredibly vivid dreams, sometimes even waking in the night with them. It hadn't taken her long to realize that if she didn't write them down while they were still fresh in her mind she'd end up losing them.

This one had been all but battered and hummed away by now. Overhead, Elizabeth and Charles were attempting to shatter the four minute mile. The ceiling sprinkled a fine mist of dust down onto the open pages of the diary. In the background the washing machine sloshed and moaned. The dream remained maddeningly out of reach.

"Emily, it's breakfast time," her mother called from the top of the stairs. "And bring the baby with you, will you, dear?"

Emily blew the plaster dust off the diary, closed it, and tucked it safely away. Albert was over by the drain when she came out. He had the lid off and was busy dropping clothespins down the hole.

"Boom," he squealed as they hit the water. "Boom."

"Boom is right, Albert. Boom on the bum, if mom sees you doing that."

"No, no, no," said Albert, shaking his head.

As she stooped to pick him up, Emily glanced down the hole to view the damage. Instantly an image from her dream flashed into her mind.

She seemed to be perched on the brink of an icy

4

abyss, feeling that she was about to fall in. Suddenly in the distance she heard a voice, a voice she knew, calling to her, warning her away.

That was all. And yet the image was so powerful that even now as she remembered it, a wave of fear washed over her. She scooped up Albert and held him tightly to her until it passed.

All the way through breakfast she kept thinking about the dream, hearing that achingly familiar voice calling her name. But it wasn't until later that day when she sat down at her diary to write it out that it suddenly struck her whose voice it had been.

It was the voice of Miss Potts.

Chapter 2

Miss Potts prodded the soft blue-gray bun of hair at the nape of her neck. Her hand strayed to the top of her head, hovered there for an instant, then with one quick pull plucked a hair.

It was a bad habit, but one Miss Potts had such a fondness for that over the years she had managed to create a considerable clearing on the top of her head. She hid it by parting her hair a little higher than she once had.

Miss Potts inspected the hair for split ends, meditatively nibbled off the root, and discarded the rest to the air. It drifted to the floor of the empty classroom.

She had been cleaning out her desk for the summer recess, when she happened to come across a story that one of her students had written for her early in the year. With lavish detail Arthur Quinn had depicted a playground where the dead walked by night. Though Miss Potts had serious reservations regarding the merit of such material, she had snapped under its spell again the instant she picked it up. Now here she was, five lurid pages later, chewing her roots and vowing not to pass the park tonight.

Suddenly the silence was shattered as the recess

bell echoed through the empty school. For an instant she swore her heart had stopped.

Miss Potts quickly skimmed the story through to its grisly end and tucked it into the top drawer of her desk. There was no doubt the boy had talent. But this fondness for corpses! She trusted that time would coax Arthur Quinn back among the living. In the meantime she must offer whatever encouragement she could. If she had learned nothing else in nearly forty years of teaching, she had learned at least that.

That was the desk done. She pushed her chair back, stood, and stretched. Though all five banks of windows were open wide, there was scarcely a breath of air in the classroom. The sun sat glaring at her from the first two rows of desks.

Earlier she had gathered her plants from the window ledges and massed them on top of the filing cabinet that flanked her desk. Already some were showing signs of recovering from the nearly complete neglect they had suffered since the end of classes, though a few more limp and yellowed leaves had fallen reprovingly to the floor.

Across the hall she could hear Mr. Murphy, the janitor, shifting desks through an open door, preparing to sand down and wax the floors. They were the only ones in the building. The rest of the teachers had done their housekeeping hurriedly during the last week of classes and were practically out the door on the heels of their students. They would not cross the school threshold again until the Labor Day weekend, when they'd tear about in an utter flap, trying to get things into some semblance of order before the hordes descended on them.

Now, however, they were off basking their bodies

on various beaches around the world. All the talk in the teachers' lounge during the final weeks of school had concerned exactly what beaches which bodies would be lying on. She had tried to be polite, but had the distinct impression that she might have a good deal more in common with Arthur Quinn and his corpses.

They considered her, of course, painfully out of date. Well, perhaps she was, she thought, as she started on the first row of desks, the row on the side of the room opposite the sun. Perhaps she was. The ritual did not vary. Patiently established over the years, it was now more or less automatic. First the blackboards, then her desk, followed by the students' desks, and finally, the supply closet. She would spend perhaps a week at it, working slowly, though she would never have considered it work, and all the while remembering. Perhaps remembering this past year, but lately more often than not remembering other years, other faces.

She finished the first desk and drew the wastebasket along beside her to the second. The desktop had been liberally scarred over the years. In the groove where one put pencils someone had scrawled "Miss Potts sucks." She made a mental note to have Mr. Murphy remove it.

She felt about the insides of the desk, finding nothing more interesting than a few discarded gum wrappers and a rolled-up magazine. It joined the wrappers at the bottom of the basket.

Her stomach growled at her. She glanced up at the clock. Not quite eleven thirty yet.

"Be still, beast," she said, and kicked the basket along to the next desk.

Empty. No, wait. Her hand brushed up against a sheet of paper wedged up against the inside of the

8

desk. She pulled it out and was about to toss it in the basket when something stopped her. She couldn't have said quite what it was, but there was something odd about the feel of the paper. She noticed now that it was brown around the edges, and brittle.

She carefully unfolded the sheet. How very strange. It appeared to be a playbill of some sort. Why, she hadn't seen one of these since she was a girl. What was it for? A magic show, it seemed. She glanced up suddenly, remembering something that had happened long ago. That memory, suddenly roused after years of quiet disregard, sent a chill ripple of fear up her spine. She read on.

Suddenly, for an instant, time fell away and she was a girl again, straining on tiptoe to read the handbill just pasted to the the pole in front of her house:

"The Mysterious Portfolio," she whispered with closed eyes. "The Ethereal Suspension." Oh, what wonders those words had awakened in her then. She had pleaded with her mother to let her go,

Please, mama, it's okay, it's not too late.
because the show was not until Saturday night, and the next day there would be church.

Please, mama.

And at last her mother had relented. For the rest of that week every time she passed the post she would stop to read the words again, strange, fantastic words that made music in her head. And if Saturday didn't hurry up and come soon she would just die.

Die.

Miss Potts opened her eyes. Her fingers, gripping the edge of the desk, were white. She stood up, overturning the wastebasket, scattering bits of crumpled paper across the floor. For an instant they

9

PROFESSOR MEPHISTO
PRESENTS
THE CHILDREN'S SHOW
■

AN EVENING OF MAGIC AND MYSTERY
consisting of incredible
FEATS OF NATURAL AND PHYSICAL MAGIC
compared with which anything before attempted
sinks into utter insignificance.

Among the features will be found
the following wondrous acts:

THE ENCHANTED CARDS
THE DECEPTIVE BALL
BIRDS OF THE PALACE
The astonishing wonder of
THE BIRTH OF FLOWERS
THE MYSTERIOUS PORTFOLIO
The seeming miracle of
THE ETHEREAL SUSPENSION
in which a child will sleep in the air.
The inexplicable
VANISHING LADY
never before seen in North America.

And concluding with
the celebrated
DECOLLATION OF JOHN THE BAPTIST
unanimously proclaimed to be the most amazing
wonder ever witnessed.

ONE NIGHT ONLY

SATURDAY, AUGUST 8th

No Money taken at the Entrance.
The Professor's Book, explanatory of his
wonderful feats, will be presented to all assistants
from the audience.

DOORS OPEN AT 7 —— SHOW BEGINS AT 8
In the Waiting Room of
THE CALEDON DEPOT

seemed like roses, spilling from a paper cone onto a stage.

She went to the window and leaned out over the sill, taking deep breaths of air, feeling the thrum of her heart against the wood.

The sun beat down on the deserted schoolyard. Her eyes wandered from one familiar object to another. The evergreen, just a seedling when she started teaching, that had now nearly grown level with the window. Mr. Murphy's battered Volkswagen, parked on the cinders by the side door. A pair of sneakers still tangled around the telephone wires. The faint remains of a game of hopscotch, chalked on the asphalt of the junior girls' yard. Her mind reached out and wrapped itself eagerly around each of them, as if to anchor itself to the world.

Gradually her heart slowed, and she turned back to the room. The handbill lay on the desk where she had left it. She scooped the scattered papers back into the basket and stood looking down at it. There was no doubt in her mind. This was the very handbill that had announced that show.

But where, after all these years, had it come from? How did it happen to get into one of her students' desks, and why?

She walked the wastebasket back to her desk and sat down, fending off the strange feeling of unreality that had settled over the room.

She did not do any further housecleaning that day. Instead, she sat for upwards of an hour at her desk, going through her Daily Record Book, studying seating plans, jotting down names and numbers. By the time she was finished she had a list of six students who had sat in that desk at one time or another during the year.

Later that day she phoned the first of them.

11

Chapter 3

On the same day Miss Potts discovered the handbill, another of her students that year, Craig Chandler, was on his way to keep a promise he had made on the last day of school. On that day Scott Renshaw, the new boy, had passed him a slip of paper with a crudely drawn map on it and a note asking Craig to look him up sometime during the summer if he had the chance.

Today Craig had followed the map all the way to the west end of town and to a seedy neighborhood he had never been in before. Now here he was, standing at the entrance to a dark and narrow dirt lane, wishing he'd lost the paper while he still had the chance.

He turned off the sweltering street and started down the lane, walking past the blank backs of buildings. Greasy bags of garbage ripened in the heat, a fan rattled in a wall, pill samples spilled from a soggy cardboard box.

He kept nervously looking back over his shoulder at the street, seeing if someone had followed him. People passed the lane entrance like ghosts, shimmering in the glaring sunlight. The sweat coursed freely down his face. He yanked up his tee shirt to wipe it off.

The lane was still puddled from last night's rain.

The storm had awakened him in the middle of the night, and for a long while he had lain there in the dark, listening to the sullen rumble of thunder in the distance and the muted whir of the fan in his mother's bedroom. When he did finally doze off again, he had the strangest dream. Something about a bombed-out room in the basement of the house, a room that hadn't been there before. And about someone in that room who was waiting for him.

This morning it had taken him nearly an hour before he felt he had securely shut out the dream, and dared to venture down the cellar stairs. There had been nothing there, of course. Nothing but the old octopus furnace silently brooding in the dark. And behind it, where the doorway had been in the dream, were dusty storm windows stacked against the wall and the water heater quietly drooling onto the concrete floor.

Shortly after breakfast he dug the piece of paper out of his back pocket. By this point it had been folded and refolded so often it was as limp as a piece of tissue paper. Right then and there he decided that this would be the day.

The lane was one of those places that look like they should never have happened. On one side of it stood the backs of the stores that faced onto Arlington Avenue. There were apartments over each store, with flat roofs and rusty fire escapes that snaked down the backs of the buildings into the dust of the lane. About the only things the shopkeepers used the lane for were parking their cars and piling their garbage. Battered trash cans with numbers painted on their sides huddled by sheetmetal doors in the slatted shade of the fire escapes. Polished cars stood mutely by them, baking in the heat.

Craig eased slowly down the lane, sidestepping

puddles, peering up at the apartment windows carved in the blank walls of the cinderblock buildings. He felt invisible faces scrutinizing him.

He clung to the side of the lane opposite the stores, the side that dropped off into the backyards of the houses on Sheldrake Street. Most of these houses were bungalows, built in the wake of the Second World War at the beginning of the baby boom. They were well-kept little houses, with checkerboard curtains in their kitchen windows and lawns that looked like they were afraid to grow too fast.

There was a low retaining wall on this side, separating the rubble and the weeds of the lane from the lawns. It was a short leap of three feet down into their clipped, green world.

As he glanced at one of the checkerboard windows, the curtain suddenly parted. For an instant Craig saw his mother's face, framed there in the glass. Then the image shifted, and he found himself staring at an old woman watering her plants.

The brief illusion had been enough, however, to spark a memory from his early childhood, something he hadn't thought about in a long time.

He had been about three or four at the time. And on nice days in the summer his mother would put him out in the backyard to play with his pail and shovel in the dirt at the end of the garden near the house.

There was a gate in the fence down by the garage, and beyond that gate, a lane. A lane not unlike this lane. And before his mother left him there to play she would always crouch down on the ground close to him, so close that he could smell her warm, sweet smell and stare down into the dark space between

14

her breasts. And almost every time he would be fooled into thinking she was going to kiss him.

But instead she would grip him firmly by the shoulders and whisper the dread warning in his ear.

"Do you see the gate, Craig?"

"Yes, mother." And he could already feel his belly ball up like a piece of crushed tin foil, and his mouth go dry.

"You know what's on the other side of that gate, don't you, darling?"

"Yes, mother." There were bad men there. Men hiding in the weedy dark between garages. Men with sharp sticks and shards of thick green glass from broken bottles, waiting for children.

"Then you won't go out there, will you, dear? You'll stay right here where mother can see you from the window and play like a nice boy, won't you?"

"Yes, mother." But playing then had been next to impossible, because he kept seeing the pale, smiling faces peeking through the slats, and the pointy sticks poking through.

It had taken him a long time to finally work up the courage to open the rusted latch on that gate one day, and creep out into the rutted lane. And nothing had happened.

Nothing.

Craig took the map from his pocket now, studied it a minute, then looked over at the last fire escape on the lane before it dead-ended into a used car lot. This was the place.

As he started up the metal stairs his stiff shoes made a twanging echo that sounded unnaturally loud. He glanced up to see that someone had set up an accordion gate at the top, securing the ends to the railing with coated wire. Looking down through

15

the grating, he found chipped bricks and broken bottles littering the ground.

As he neared the top of the stairs he froze suddenly and almost lost his balance. A face was staring through the gate. Then a pudgy arm, clutching a popsicle, reached through and he realized it was only a little boy, standing there watching him. As he straddled the gate the little boy looked up at him curiously, then turned and toddled off down the breezeway, diapers drooping. He disappeared through a door with a torn screen.

Three apartments opened onto the breezeway, one on either side and one facing him at the far end. A fan had been wedged in the open window of that apartment. It sat there blowing the dead air around in the dark.

He could smell the creosote seeping off the boards of the breezeway. Midway down it, an umbrella clothesline stood with its post anchored in a hole in one of the planks. It was laden with diapers, hanging limp and motionless in the heat.

The scattered corpses of June bugs littered the boards. As he crossed to the first door on the left, according to the instructions on the sheet, Craig felt a telling crunch beneath his shoe, but he did not bother to look.

He knocked twice on the door. The sound seemed hollow to him, as though the apartment on the other side were empty, and he wondered for a moment if he had the right place. He was about to fish the paper out of his pocket again, when the door suddenly opened.

And there stood Scott Renshaw, naked save for the towel around his waist.

"Well, well. Look who's here. You're not going to believe this, Craig, but I was just thinking about

16

you today. Hey, come on in. Park yourself someplace while I get something on. Have any trouble finding the place?''

"No. No trouble at all." Craig followed Scott into the dimness of the apartment. "I would have phoned first, but I didn't have the number."

"Don't worry about it," said Scott. He crossed the room, rubbing himself with the towel, and disappeared through a door. His narrow retreating form looked almost skeletal.

The drapes were drawn. The only light came from a large aquarium where angel fish drifted elegantly around a submerged ceramic wreck. Craig edged slowly into the room, absorbing it, feeling everything tinged vaguely with unreality, as if a sudden motion might cause it all to disappear.

The damp heat, coupled with the green light from the aquarium, made it momentarily seem as though vines and creepers had grown over everything. The bed was unmade. Clothes spilled from half-shut dresser drawers and were strewn about the floor. Model planes with spiked jaws decaled on their noses hung semianimate from the ceiling.

He sat down on the edge of the bed, straining to read the titles of the books on the shelf beside it. They were books on magic, of course. Scott ate, slept, and breathed magic. The lower shelf was crammed with magical paraphernalia: decks of cards, linking rings, lengths of rope, cups and balls and colored boxes. Tools of the trade.

He could hear Scott coming down the hall now, whistling. He sat up on the bed and suddenly caught sight of his reflection in the dresser mirror in front of him.

And then an incredible thing happened. It was as if the image rippled suddenly, like a piece of painted scenery in a play. And when it settled again he found himself staring at a totally different room. It was barren and devastated. Hunks of plaster dangled from the wall, leaving the lathing gaping through like bone. The walls were covered in crayon scrawl.

He swung around. Scott was standing in the doorway, buttoning his shirt, and staring at him. The room was as it had been before.

"Hey, are you all right?"

"Yeah, fine. You startled me, that's all." What *was* that?

"So I noticed." Scott was standing in front of the dresser mirror now, combing his damp hair straight back off his face in soft spikes. Craig sat with his hands tucked between his knees, watching. It had been that way from the beginning, him watching Scott. Ever since that day he'd first seen him in the schoolyard. There was something about him that he found irresistable. He'd felt it even back then—the almost palpable aura of darkness and mystery that surrounded Scott. It spoke to a need so deep inside him that he had barely known it was there. It was as though he'd been waiting all his life for someone like Scott to come along and find him.

At first sight he seemed like just another shy, quiet kid, a loner like himself, the kind of a kid who almost invited abuse. But just one glance from those dark, hooded eyes of his, one flicker of a smile from that full, brooding mouth, and you knew that there was more, much more.

Frankie Grogan had learned that—the hard way.

Chapter 4

It was some time around the beginning of May that Scott Renshaw had suddenly appeared on the scene. It was hot, the end of school was in sight, and Frankie Grogan and his gang were getting restless and bored. Craig considered himself more than a little lucky at having avoided the attention of the Grogan gang all year, but right about now he could feel his luck rapidly running out.

He was sitting by himself on the bench by the water fountain one morning, pretending to read, but keeping one eye fixed firmly on Frankie and the boys, when he suddenly noticed a boy he had never seen before over by the fence. The boy was walking alongside the fence, running a stick across the steel mesh as he went. Now and then he'd pause, look out indifferently over the noisy yard, then start in pacing again. Back and forth, back and forth, like a leopard locked in a cage. As he sat there watching him, Craig felt his fear of the gang edge quietly aside and an odd fascination for this stranger take its place.

Each day the following week he reappeared. It was always the same; one minute there'd be no sign of him at all, and then suddenly he'd be standing by the fence, as if he'd just stepped out of nowhere. Sometimes he'd pace, sometimes just stand there leaning with one leg up against the fence and his hands pushed down into his pockets. No one ever went near him.

Eventually the bell would ring, the groups break up, the bodies slowly start to drain into the school. He'd just stand there watching them. Craig would linger by the bench as long as he could, then have to rush to make the last of the line as the boy turned and wandered off.

Then one morning he failed to appear. Two, three days went by, with still no sign of him. Craig found himself feeling strangely dejected. It was as though some secret bond between them had been severed. There was a sudden emptiness inside him. Fear of the Grogan gang rushed in to fill the void.

At the side of the school there was a stairwell, leading down to the boiler room. People called it "the pit." It was isolated and out of sight and the janitor never used it. Frankie and the gang would duck down there for a smoke between classes or to escape gym. It was also the place they used for their shakedowns.

Twice in the past week kids had been targeted and taken down. Usually the gang was after money, but sometimes they were just looking for a little fun. Only one guy, usually Frankie, would go down with the victim. He'd put his arm around the kid as though they were real good friends, and then he'd lead him right down those stairs. The rest of the gang would stand around the railing at the top and stare out into the schoolyard, making sure no one came in sight of the slaughter.

In a few minutes Frankie would reappear, strutting up the stairs in his cleated boots, snapping up the wind flap on his leather jacket. The gang would close around him like a bunch of drones around the

20

queen bee, and they'd saunter off through the schoolyard, hands hooked in their pockets. Now and then they'd break out laughing, and you knew Frankie had said something cute.

It would usually take another few minutes before the victim made his way out of the pit. In the meantime no one went near. To go anywhere near there meant that you knew what had happened, and if you knew what had happened then you felt like a real creep that you hadn't done anything to stop it.

One day, about a week after the boy by the fence had disappeared, there was a knock at the classroom door. Miss Potts asked Craig to get it. He opened the door and almost fell over on his face.

It was him. Up close his clothes looked rumpled and worn and his face seemed incredibly pale. He didn't say a word. He just flashed Craig a flicker of a smile and stepped past him into the room. He had a note in his hand that he gave to Miss Potts. She read it over a couple of times, then introduced the new pupil to the class. His name was Scott Renshaw and he had just moved here from out of town. He was assigned a seat near the back of the class.

It became almost immediately obvious that Scott Renshaw wanted nothing whatever to do with school. He just sat there at his desk, running his finger back and forth along the pencil groove and eyeing the clock. Occasionally he'd reach into his pocket and pull out a dog-eared deck of cards. For the first few days Miss Potts did her best to involve him in the class, but whenever she spoke to him he would just fix her with one of his stares and smile a little. No one in the world could smile like Scott Renshaw. It was like a crack opening in the earth. Eventually she just gave up.

In the schoolyard people kept their distance from

Scott, as they would from a strange dog that might suddenly bite. He spent most of the time sitting on the concrete steps, playing with those cards of his, and doing amazing things with them. Craig would sit as near as he could without seeming obvious, just to watch him.

One morning as he sat there spellbound, watching Scott apparently pluck cards from thin air, he glanced up and noticed Frankie and the boys walking toward them. Frankie was in the lead and the others were sauntering along casually behind him. He caught Craig's eye and winked.

Craig felt the ground fall away from under him and his stomach leap up into his throat. Pure panic washed over him. Should he run? He shot a quick look toward the fence at the end of the yard. There was no way he could make it before they caught up to him. And Frankie would make him pay for the extra effort. He resigned himself to the inevitable.

But when the gang was about ten yards away from him something happened. Renshaw suddenly glanced up from his cards and saw them coming. He got to his feet, carefully tucked the cards into his pocket, and ambled over to where Craig was sitting. He just stationed himself there between Craig and the gang, and smiled. Not a big broad smile, just a little flicker, like someone peeking out from behind a curtain.

The gang stopped dead in their tracks. Nothing like this had ever happened before. It took Frankie a few seconds to react, and when he did, he laughed. It sounded like he didn't mean it.

"Okay, wise guy," he said.

Renshaw didn't give Frankie a chance to put his arm around him. He just turned and started walking

22

toward the side of the building. It was like Scott was leading them.

By this time a crowd had begun to gather. But as they rounded the corner of the building, with Frankie and the boys in the lead, there was no sign of Renshaw. Frankie must have figured he'd run off. He picked up a pop bottle and hurled it high in the air, and you could see the relief written all over his face. But just as the bottle came crashing down against the asphalt of the girls' yard, they heard laughter from the pit.

If Craig had been alone he would have run when he heard that sound. It reminded him of the time he'd been crawling around under the bridge by the old depot, when from way back in the shadows near the top he'd heard the same sound. Later he'd convinced himself that it must have been one of the old men who camped out under there. But at the time he was sure that that laugh had belonged to something inhuman, something that wasn't going to let him get away from there.

The circle dissolved, and Frankie was left alone staring over at the pit. There was nothing coming from there now. Not a sound. As Frankie edged his way slowly over there, he glanced back over his shoulder once or twice, as if for reassurance. He looked like a little kid lost in the dark.

When he got to the top of the stairs he stopped dead. It looked for a second like he was going to run. And then he started down, slowly.

It was a long time before anyone walked up out of there. Renshaw was the first to reappear. He looked around him, as if he couldn't quite figure out why everyone was standing there, and then he started walking away through the yard. He was as far as the fence when the bell rang. Craig stood over by the stairs watching him while the others made their way into the school. When the last of the line had disappeared inside and the doors had swung shut, he was still watching. Scott had left the yard by then and was slowly disappearing down the street. Craig took one last look over his shoulder at the heavy wooden doors of the school, then turned and started after him.

Frankie didn't hang out with the gang anymore after that day. He just kind of kept to himself, and you had the feeling that something had gone wrong with him. Well before the end of the year he just disappeared. But before he did he said something one day. It didn't seem to make much sense at the time. He said that Renshaw had shown him something down there in the pit that day. That was all. He'd shown him something.

That had been the beginning. And as he sat in the dim room now, still watching Scott in the mirror, Craig realized for the first time that all that had followed since had led smoothly and somehow inevitably to this. There had never been any choice really.

It was still a mystery to him why Scott had bothered to save him that day, just as it was a mystery what had happened between him and Frankie down there. But then everything about Scott was ultimately a mystery. Someday, though, if he was just patient, Craig was convinced he would learn the answers. Already he knew one thing for certain, that wherever it lay, the key to the mystery was magic.

Chapter 5

Miss Potts hung up the phone and ran her pencil slowly through the fourth name on her list. This was not getting any easier. She had not yet found a way of asking about the handbill that did not make her sound slightly crazy. The reactions of those she'd spoken to so far were the same. First surprise, followed by silence, and, finally, a wary reserve. Come fall, she would have won herself quite a reputation. She chased the unpleasant thought from her mind like a cat from the sitting room, and closed the book.

There was, she was sure, a perfectly logical explanation for the handbill being in the desk. She was simply overreacting. Perhaps, after all, it was not even the same show she had seen. Fifty years was a long time. The mind played tricks.

There was a knock at her door. "Miss Potts?" It was Mr. Palmer, a fellow boarder in the house.

"Yes, Mr. Palmer. What is it?"

"Dinnertime, Miss Potts. Miss Blight has called you twice now."

"Oh, I'm sorry. I was just on the phone. I'll be right down."

Miss Blight, who owned the house, occupied the ground floor and rented out the upper rooms. Miss Potts shared the second floor with Mrs. Holmes, the widow who rented the large front room that had once been the master bedroom. Mr. Palmer inhabited the third floor, two rooms with sloped ceilings reached by a steep narrow stairway beside the bathroom.

Miss Potts was the most recent arrival. Though she had lived there for nearly fifteen years, she was still considered the junior member of the group.

Dinner in the house was a formal affair. Mr. Palmer put on his school tie and sometimes pinned his military bars to the breast pocket of his jacket. He had been an officer in the war. Mrs. Holmes wore one of the apparently endless collection of dresses in her wardrobe, and rouged her lips.

The four of them would gather in the dining room at six sharp for a long leisurely meal, after which Mr. Palmer would read to them from the paper while Mrs. Holmes clucked her tongue reprovingly at the world.

Miss Potts found the after-dinner sessions increasingly difficult. Despite her gray hairs and the pain that gripped her knee on damp days, she felt that she did not quite fit. A lifetime of teaching children had perhaps left her younger than the others.

For them the house sufficed. Nothing changed within the confines of its walls. The furniture sat in precisely the same spots it had forty years ago. The radio remained fixed on the same station. Among themselves they had quietly decided that the world was not quite the place it had been once.

Dinner tonight was liver. Miss Potts, already unsettled by the day's events, was still struggling heroically to coax a few mouthfuls down her throat. Mr. Palmer put on his glasses and started to peruse the paper.

"Fire today," he announced.

"Oh, where was that?" asked Mrs. Holmes, dabbing at the corners of her mouth with a napkin. Mrs. Holmes was fond of fires, bless her scorched heart.

"Over on Shuter Street. One of the flop houses near the mission."

"Oh, I see." She had instantly lost interest. It was one of *those* places.

"Fat," said Mr. Palmer.

Miss Blight, who was sensitive about her weight, looked up from her liver drippings. "Pardon me?" she said.

"Fat fire. It says here it was a fat fire."

There was a pause while old minds registered information. Miss Potts pushed the liver from the near to the far side of her plate with her fork and speared another limp strand of onion. Disgusting stuff, liver. Enough to turn one into a raging vegetarian.

Mr. Palmer turned the page. "Another article on the old depot," he announced. Miss Potts looked up. "It seems the paper is throwing its support behind the historical society's idea of renovating it. They urge the town council to approve the final phase of the plan when they meet next month."

"As well they should," remarked Mrs. Holmes. "It's nothing short of disgraceful the way they've let the place deteriorate. Anything would be an improvement."

"What is it they have in mind for the building?" asked Miss Blight. "Something about a museum, wasn't it?"

"Yes," said Mr. Palmer. "That's right. They plan to turn it into a railway museum."

Miss Potts rose suddenly from the table. She had tried to take another piece of liver, this time burying it in a wad of mashed potato in a bid to sneak it past the sentry at the back of her throat. Without success. She excused herself and went to flush it down the toilet.

"Why, look," said Mrs. Holmes, when she had gone. "She hardly touched her dinner."

"Looked a little peaked," remarked Mr. Palmer as he turned the page.

Miss Potts closed the door of her room behind her and turned the key. It was a pretty room, the prettiest in the house as far as she was concerned. It had a high molded ceiling, a lovely old canopy bed, and a rounded bay window with a window seat.

Some might consider it small, but Miss Potts found it more than adequate. Had it been any larger she would have felt lost in it, like a grain of rice sealed inside a gourd. As it was, there were no bare spaces about to make her feel hollow. That comforted her somehow, especially now.

The room was at the rear of the house. Her window overlooked a long, narrow yard, flanked by tall poplars on either side. Beyond the yard lay an untenanted lot, railway land, an undulating field of waist-high grass and weed. The field was intersected by an ancient railway line, the roadbed rising above the weeds like the smooth mottled back of an enormous snake. Nestled against the track, facing her, just before the field fell away into the green scar of the Bedford ravine, stood the old Caledon Depot.

The station had been built before the turn of the century and had about it a certain whimsy peculiar to the late Victorian period of architecture. At one end of the depot there was a waiting room, above which rose a steeply pitched conical roof, like a witch's cap. Two elongated windows in the wall of the waiting room looked out onto a platform, commanding a view of the track as well. Shuttered now, they looked like eyelids lowered in sleep.

Beside the waiting room, in the center of the building, stood the ticket office, its bay window jutting out onto the platform to allow the station operator a clear view of oncoming traffic. At the far end of the building was a baggage room.

Rising from the roof above the ticket office and the baggage room were a set of three small dormer windows. These rooms at one time had been accommodations for travelers stopping over in town.

Against the wall of the station stood a bench protected from the weather by the wide, sweeping eaves of the roof. Ornamental brackets supported the eaves, the coiled scroll-work resembling the slumbering shapes of dragons.

In the angle of the gable above the ticket office window the carpenter had created a wooden sunburst effect. That sunburst was a sunset now. The Caledon Depot had not seen a passenger in its waiting room for nearly thirty years. The windows were boarded shut, and the entrance from the platform permanently locked against vandals. Time had curled and blistered the ancient paint upon its clapboard walls. The roof shingles were warped. Some had come loose and blown away. Fingers of moss crept up from the eaves.

Miss Potts fetched her bag from the closet and went to sit down on the window seat. The bag was a pathetic-looking thing. One handle was attached with twine and the zipper had jammed so that it would no longer shut. With obvious reluctance she reached in and drew out her Daily Record Book.

As she fanned through the pages, the handbill fell out onto the window seat. She stared down at it for

29

a second with something like surprise, as though she'd more than half expected it to have vanished since she put it there this morning.

The brittleness she'd noticed at first had become worse, and as she unfolded the sheet now, one discolored corner flaked off and fluttered to the floor.

Fifteen minutes later Miss Blight puffed up the stairs with a tray of tea and shortbreads. She knocked lightly on Miss Potts's door, catching her breath. Receiving no reply, she decided that Miss Potts must have lain down for a nap. She left the tray by the door and went back to join the others.

Miss Potts lay fully clothed across the bed. Her head moved slowly from side to side and she was murmuring something in her sleep.

Fifty years had fallen away. She was a little girl again, walking through the open door of the Caledon Depot, her father by her side. It was almost eight o'clock, and the Children's Show was about to begin.

Chapter 6

The Children's Show

I

The children sat in a semicircle before the stage. It was a hot August evening and the windows had been thrown open to circulate the air. Nonetheless, a couple of the younger ones had fallen asleep upon obliging laps. The sound of their breathing blended with the muted trill of the crickets outside and the chatter of the parents milling about at the back of the room.

It was a makeshift stage. Four squat barrels with planks laid across them, and a piece of patched velvet suspended between two poles as a backdrop. In the center of the stage stood a table draped with a satin cloth upon which mysterious symbols had been embroidered in gold. To either side stood braziers of burning coals, filling the air with thick scented smoke that curled and crept about the stage.

Slowly from the midst of the smoke a figure seemed to form, the long limbs twisting, bending in the breeze, the face a drift of smoke. A collective gasp went up from the crowd, and suddenly, there before them stood the magician.

31

"Mirrors," whispered one parent knowingly to another, and smiled.

At first glance he appeared almost comical. His lips were far too red, his face too pale, as though it had been dusted with powder. His eyebrows and sideburns were too dark, too defined, as if they had been pencilled in.

But as he slowly advanced to center stage, something in his manner, something in the look with which he fixed the crowd, caught the children's breath and stopped it in their throats. His eyes had an almost supernatural intensity. They bored into theirs, as though they could plumb their very souls. Each child in the room felt that they were utterly alone with him. It was frightening, yet at the same time curiously alluring.

It seemed an eternity that he stood there, slowly peeling off his gloves, saying nothing. Meanwhile, from the back of the room the whispering continued. The magician stared out over the children's heads in the direction of the sound. Then he held the gloves high in the air over his head.

There was a sudden blur, a beating of wings, and a pair of doves fluttered across the room and perched on the rafters above the parents' heads. The children craned their heads around, following their flight.

The magician sauntered to the edge of the stage. "Well, well," he said. "And what do we have here? There are either some very large children back there by the door, or else some adults have decided to attend the show."

Peels of relieved laughter sounded through the room. The parents smiled back nervously. One of them coughed.

"Now it seems to me," continued the magician,

32

his voice laced with ice, "that at any given time there are any number of entertainments in town especially for the adults." He turned to the children huddled by the stage. "And are you children allowed to attend those?"

An emphatic no came up from the crowd.

"In that case, doesn't it seem only fair that the adults should be forbidden to attend a children's show?"

"Yes," yelled the children delightedly.

He cupped one hand to his ear. "I'm afraid I couldn't quite hear you."

"Yes!" they shouted, waking the two little ones who had fallen asleep. They sat up and rubbed their eyes.

"Well then, I suggest that you all turn around, gaze very intently at the adults, and think powerful thoughts. And perhaps to begin this evening's show we can make them disappear."

The children turned as one to stare fixedly at the small group standing huddled in the shadows by the door. Silence fell over the room, broken only by the beating of wings as the birds flew down from the rafters and swooped about the parents' heads. Only now they were no longer doves, but large black birds. The door opened, and one by one the parents filed out of the room. More than one paused and looked back a little anxiously at the smiling figure on the stage.

Then the door swung shut, the birds settled back in the rafters, and in the hush that followed, the show began. . . .

Chapter 7

It was Saturday morning. Elizabeth and Charles were in the living room, skydiving from the couch. The TV was screaming at the top of its tubes to no one in particular. Albert, who five minutes earlier had vroomed his toy truck into Emily's ankle, was in his crib now, wailing. The truck was lying at the foot of the basement stairs, where it had landed when she kicked it from the top. Emily went to put the kettle on for a strong pot of tea.

"Stop that jumping in there." There was a momentary lull followed by a fit of muffled giggles. The giggling irritated her worse than the jumping.

"And turn down that television. No one's watching it anyway. Better still, turn it off."

The TV was tuned in to a show on sports car racing. Mom had put it on to keep Albert amused. Albert was going through that phase when he was absolutely entranced by anything that had wheels and made noise. Mind you, Walter next door was nearly nineteen and still locked into that phase, probably permanently. He practically slept with the '79 Chevy he had up on blocks in his garage. Albert, predictably, had become bored with the set once the race was over, and had gone back to his killer dump truck.

Dad had picked the truck out for him one day

when he was down at the hobby shop, admiring the latest shipment of narrow-guage railroad engines they'd received. The truck was meant to sit peacefully on a hobbyist's shelf, collecting dust. Single-handedly, Albert had turned it into an instrument of destruction.

Everything that existed about three inches above ground level was in peril. The door frames wore red gashes from the bumper paint, the furniture legs were gouged, and mother had bandages on both ankles. The truck was thrown away an average of ten times a day. But the sound of Albert screaming was worse than the battle scars. He was screaming now, and slamming his head against the end of the crib from the sounds of it.

Emily clapped the lid down on the teapot and banged down the basement stairs to get the truck. It was lying belly up on the floor by the washing machine. There was no sign of damage. You probably couldn't have destroyed the thing if you tried.

She wiped the truck off with the damp rag draped over the laundry tubs and headed back upstairs. The racket from the bedroom had stopped. She went in to check. Albert was lying on his side in a corner of the crib with his thumb in his mouth. How could someone who looked so angelic when he was asleep be such a terror the rest of the time? He probably wouldn't sleep a wink this afternoon, she thought, but this afternoon was several hours away. Right now she needed a few minutes of relative calm.

She poured the tea into one of the few cups that still had a matching saucer, and sat down at the kitchen table. In the front room Elizabeth and Charles lay transfixed in front of the tube. Bugs Bunny had just come on, which meant they were as good as gone for the next half hour, barring commercials.

Mother had driven dad down to the old train depot. He and a couple of the other members of the Caledon Historical Society had volunteered to work on the initial phase of the cleanup of the place over the summer. The building had been slated for demolition for the past five years, but the society contended that the depot was of historic value and should be saved. They had managed to rally enough community support that it seemed as though their plan to restore the depot and turn it into a railway museum might succeed. Father, on learning of the newspaper's support for the scheme last night, had been ecstatic. He had had a lot to do with the society's success. Railroads and all that pertained to them were his passion.

It had all started with the model train set he had been given as a kid. Over the years it had quietly grown as he added new track, cars, and engines, and began constructing landscapes for the layout from papier-mâché and paint.

As the collection grew, and the family with it, he had been forced to move it from one corner of the house to another, each move necessitating a complete dismantling and rebuilding of the layout. Up until last summer it had been housed in the basement. Then one Saturday morning Elizabeth and Charles had made their way downstairs while everyone was still asleep.

You never got a straight story on exactly whose idea it had been, but one of them decided it would be kind of neat to dismantle the matchstick fences, gather up the plaster cows that were scattered over the landscape, and plug one end of the tunnel with the stuff. Then they both sat back and started up the trains.

It was a neat idea, all right. The southbound train came roaring along the track, rounded a corner, and disappeared into the tunnel. About two seconds later matchsticks and cows exploded from the other end, the train emerged, jumped the track, and went crashing into the side of the furnace. Meanwhile, one of the cows landed on the northbound track. Along came the train. It hit the cow, jumped the rail, and went slamming into the side of the platform, injuring three wooden people who were standing there waiting for the train.

At this point they heard father coming and barricaded themselves in the cold room.

Father didn't say a word. He took one look at the devastation, walked up the stairs and out the side door in his slippers, and went to the garage. He backed the car out, drove it around to the front, and parked it at the curb in front of the house. Then he went back to the basement, methodically dismantled the layout for the last time, and moved it piece by piece out to the garage. It took about three hours, and Elizabeth and Charles didn't budge from the cold room the whole time it was going on.

Since then the railroad had remained in the garage under lock and key, while the car stayed parked out front, quietly rusting. It wasn't doing the car a whole lot of good, but it had probably saved Elizabeth's and Charles's lives.

The phone rang. Charles groaned and went to get it, his eyes still glued to the set.

"Hello?"

"Hello," whispered the voice on the other end, "may I please speak to Emily?"

"Who is this?" asked Charles.

"I'm afraid you wouldn't know me, dear. My name is Irma. What's yours?"

"Charles. Hey, why are you whispering? Are you sick or something?"

"Well, not exactly, Charles. It's rather a long story. Is Emily there?"

Charles's response to this was to scream for Emily and drop the receiver onto the coffee table. He went back to his cartoons.

"Some weird lady on the phone for you," he said as she came into the room. Emily picked up the phone.

"Hello?" she said.

"Hello, Emily?"

"Yes, who is this?"

"This is Irma Potts, Emily."

"Miss Potts?"

"Yes, that's right. From the school."

"Will you hold the line for a minute, Miss Potts?" Emily clapped her hand over the receiver and tucked it under her arm. It was Miss Potts, all right. But why on earth was she whispering? She could hardly hear her over the din of the TV.

"Will you two turn that thing down. I'm trying to talk."

Elizabeth elbowed her way up to the set, reached up, and turned it down a touch. Emily picked up the phone and walked the cord to its full length. It made it just inside the kitchen doorway. Leaning against the doorjamb, she took the receiver from under her arm.

"Sorry, Miss Potts, I couldn't hear you very well."

"Yes, my dear. I must apologize for whispering. But I don't want the others to hear. They think I'm

sleeping. Oh, wait. I think I hear someone coming."
There was silence for a few seconds. "No, it's all right. Just Mr. Palmer going up to his room. Are you still there, Emily?"

"Yes. I'm still here." Boy, Miss Potts had always been a little strange, but not this strange.

"The reason I'm calling, Emily, is that I have stumbled upon a bit of a mystery and I thought perhaps you might be able to help me with it. Yesterday I was cleaning out the students' desks at school and I came across something in one of them. An old handbill. For a magic show. You wouldn't know anything about it, I suppose?"

Miss Potts anticipated the silence that followed. Next would come the hurried denial of any knowledge.

"Actually, Miss Potts, I think I might know something about a handbill. But—" She was not given the chance to finish what she was going to say. Miss Potts interrupted her, obviously excited.

"Emily, I must talk to you. But not now, on the phone. Do you think you could meet me this afternoon? In the park near the library at around two o'clock?"

"Yes, but—"

"Good. I'll explain everything then. I must go now. Goodbye, Emily."

There was a click, and the line went dead. Emily stood looking down at the receiver for a few seconds, and then quietly hung up the phone.

Bugs Bunny was winding down, and Elizabeth and Charles were starting to come round. Five minutes later she heard the car cough up to the curb. She ran to wake up Albert before mother got in.

As the side door opened, Emily was casually standing at the sink, rinsing out her cup. Albert was leaning against the stove, slack-jawed and sweaty, wondering what had happened to him.

Chapter 8

It was nearly twenty past two by the clock over the drugstore door. Emily stood with the stroller on the corner across from the park, waiting for the light to change. A girl in tennis whites was waiting too, swinging her racket as if she was serving, bouncing up and down on the balls of her feet. Albert was looking at her as if she'd just landed.

The girl suddenly noticed them standing beside her. The racket dropped abruptly to her side and she went down on her heels. Her face settled into the flat expression of someone who suddenly finds herself in a room with the wrong sort of people.

The stroller was, admittedly, not a thing of beauty. Having survived the last three Endicott children, it had definitely entered the twilight of life. It was difficult to tell whether the frame was a rusty chrome or a chromey rust. The seat cover was held together with large black patches of electrical tape. The hubcaps had long since popped loose and been lost. It looked like it wanted nothing so much as to be left in peace in its own little rust-stained space on the porch.

The girl took one look at it and edged away, dangling the toes of her sneakers over the curb, waiting for the light to change. As soon as it did, she fluttered across the road, pink pompoms bobbing at the backs of her sneakers, and disappeared down the stairs into the park. She was long gone by the time Emily reached the stairs and began bumping the stroller down.

The shallow flagstone steps led past a series of terraces as they descended into the park. At the bottom there was a bicycle path, trees, and a tennis court.

The first terrace was a paved area bordered by a low iron fence. Paths led past patterned gardens. Ranks of rose bushes stood in solemn rows. There were benches here and there where you could sit and watch them wilting in the heat.

In the center of this open area stood the statue of Peter Pan. He was perched upon a rough granite pedestal, blowing on his horn and calling the children away. He had been there a long time, and had gone slightly green from the blowing. No one seemed to be listening.

At the far end of the terrace, on a bench overlooking a topiary, sat a woman wearing sunglasses and a large straw hat. The woman was watching the gardener shaping the ears of a bush bunny with his shears. The gardener looked hot and bored with the whole business. He nipped at the ears as if he'd just love for the shears to slip and send the leafy head falling to the manicured lawn at his feet.

Once they reached the terrace, Albert, who until now had been more or less numbed by the heat, spotted a drinking fountain and came to life.

"Dink! Dink!" he wailed, struggling against the plastic harness and slamming his shoes against the metal footrest. It sounded like someone doing drum rolls on a garbage can lid. The gardener glanced up.

"Okay, Albert, you can have a drink. Just calm

down for a second." Emily knelt down and started struggling with the strap. Mother had done one of her extra special knots on it—as if she wasn't too sure she was going to let him out again.

It had been one of those mornings. As soon as mother had arrived home from dropping Mr. Endicott at the depot she had started in on the housework. Elizabeth and Charles were banished down the street with their bicycles and a fistful of popsicles to lure the neighborhood children from their television sets. Albert, dressed in his sunsuit and a big blue hat, was put on the front porch with the big box of toys from the basement.

That had worked for approximately ten minutes, by which time Albert had emptied the box and hurled the toys over the railing onto the walk. Emily was still standing at the sink, up to her neck in suds, when there came the familiar sound of Albert's shoes slamming against the screen door.

"In! Albert come in!" By the time she got to him he had succeeded in yanking his sun hat, which he hated, off his head. It dangled in front of his face like a feed bag.

"What do you mean you want to come in, Albert? You just got out. If I bring you in, the next thing I know you'll be screaming to go out again. Why don't you just stay out there and play nicely for a little while, until mama and Emmy finish working, all right?"

Albert paused for a second and thought that over. Then he started screaming again. It wasn't that he didn't understand. It was just that he wasn't buying it.

"In! Albert come in!" He had scrambled to his feet and was standing with his face flattened against the screen. From the back bedroom came the sound

43

of the vacuum cleaner, banging up against the baseboards, and the radio that followed mother around the house, screaming over the wheeze.

"Tell you what, Albert. If you stay out there and be good, I'll give you a popsicle. How about that?"

It was like you had slammed a lid down on top of him. The silence was automatic and absolute. He pushed off the limp screen and sat down with a muffled thud amidst the wreckage of the porch. All the way to the fridge Emily prayed there would be another popsicle left.

There was. She snapped it in half against the edge of the counter and took it out to him. There was no way you could give Albert half at a time. He knew there were two of them, and he wanted them both—now.

"Here you go, Albert." She pushed the halves into his outstretched hands, tied a bib around his neck, and twisted the sunbonnet back on top of his head.

"And try not to make a mess. Please?" It was a ridiculous thing to say.

Half an hour later mother had worked her way into the small bedroom off the living room, where Elizabeth and Charles slept. The dishes were nearly done, and Albert hadn't made so much as a peep.

Suddenly Elizabeth burst through the side door with Charles in hot pursuit. Charles had been throwing dirt bombs at Mrs. Rutledge's door, she said. Mrs. Rutledge had come out and said she was going to phone the police.

"I never threw nothing at the old bag's door," said Charles. "Joey done it."

"Did it," said mother. She shut them both in their bedroom. It was then she noticed the mud they had tracked through her clean house.

When she went to throw their shoes out onto the front porch she discovered Albert happily splashing in a popsicle puddle, his bonnet twisted down in front of his face, his hair a mass of sticky spikes.

Two minutes later the phone rang. Mrs. Rutledge had quite a sense of timing. Mother listened for about a minute, then quietly put the receiver down.

All of which served to explain the knot which Emily, with the aid of her teeth, had finally managed to work loose. As soon as he was free Albert scrambled out of the stroller and made for the fountain.

Miss Potts sat at the far end of the bench, fanning herself with a folded paper. She had chosen the bench with a purpose. It was the only one in shade. However, the shade was steadily receding. The sun had already claimed her gray bag on the bench beside her. In a few more minutes she would have to move.

A child was putting up a fuss over there in the general direction of the stairs. The child was, she supposed, that small bluish blur, and its mother that narrow whitish one in front of it. They could not be trees or bushes, for they were moving. Still, there was no point in staring; blurs they were, and blurs they would remain. She faced frontwards again, fanning herself, still trying to remember what she had done with her glasses. They were definitely not in the bag. She had turned it out twice on the bench since she arrived, looking for them. They were no doubt on her dresser, where she had likely set them down when she tried on the sunglasses Mrs. Holmes had lent her.

The sunglasses were an absolute necessity against the glare of the sun. Her sleep last night had been fitful, a jumble of disjointed images from that magic

45

show so long ago. And running like a thread through them all, the magician's own lilting voice, droning on and on. In the end he had leaped down from the stage, floating through the air and landing noiselessly beside her. Fixing her with those deep beseeching eyes of his, he had reached out and stroked her cheek.

She woke up instantly, her head pounding and her heart racing, to discover that she had fallen asleep without undressing. She waited for a long while for the dream to fall away, then rose and slowly undressed in the dark. She could still feel the touch of that chill hand on her cheek and see the hunger in those eyes. It was all too real. She dared not turn on the light, lest she find him standing by the window, watching.

The room was gray with dawn before she managed to fall asleep again. She did not go down to breakfast this morning. The headache was still with her. She kept the blinds drawn against the light, which only made it worse, and remained in bed on Miss Blight's orders. It was only by doing so that she escaped their phoning the doctor. It was while she was supposed to be resting that she had called Emily.

Now, across the irregular flagstones of the terrace she heard the rusty squeal of something approaching on wheels.

"Miss Potts?" The voice was familiar.

She leaned forward, squinting. "Emily Endicott? Is that you? You must forgive me, my dear, but I've mislaid my glasses and I can't see a thing without them."

Albert had scrambled up onto the bench beside her.

"Lo," he said.

"Why, hello," said Miss Potts. "And what's your name?"

Albert didn't like to be asked his name. He looked at her for a second and then made a lunge for the sunglasses.

"This is Albert," explained Emily. "My little brother. I hope you don't mind my having brought him along."

"No, not at all."

Albert caught sight of the gardener and rushed over to the iron railing. "Lo," he yelled down through the fence. The gardener tried to ignore him. This was exactly the wrong approach. A chorus of steadily more vocal hellos followed. At last the gardener gave up and said hello back. He took off his straw hat, wiped his brow with a rumpled hanky, and stepped back to survey his work.

He'd trimmed it a little too much. There was a sizable gap in the greenery around the rabbit's middle. Branches showed like bones through the opening. He picked his shears up off the lawn and moved on to the poodle.

"I must apologize for hanging up on you this morning. Mrs. Holmes was at my door and I was supposed to have been too ill to be talking on the phone. Needless to say, they were none too pleased to see me up and about this afternoon. Mr. Palmer practically demanded that he accompany me."

She saw the look of confusion on Emily's face.

"But of course, you don't know Mr. Palmer or Mrs. Holmes. They are fellow boarders in the house where I live."

"I didn't know that you were sick, Miss Potts."

"Well, sick is perhaps too strong a word. I had a bit of an upset yesterday, and I haven't felt quite

47

like myself since. But after speaking to you this morning I've already begun to feel much better."

She was busy now rooting about in the large gray bag beside her on the bench. Emily looked over at Albert. He was sitting on the ground with his head resting against the railing, sucking his thumb. His eyes were half-shut and he was obviously ready for a nap. But if she dared to lay him down he would scream blue murder. Albert did not like to go to sleep. Sleep came to him. It was creeping up behind him right now.

"Ah, here it is." Miss Potts squirmed as far as possible into the security of the shade. Still, her hands were washed with sunlight as she held out the folded handbill to Emily. "I believe this is yours," she said.

Emily took the paper. It was obviously very old, as Miss Potts had told her. It had begun to crack along the fold lines. This could not possibly be the same handbill. She opened it carefully, and discovered to her surprise that it was. The words at any rate were the same. She remembered the name, Professor Mephisto. She glanced over at Albert. He had fallen asleep against the railing, his mouth stoppered shut with his thumb.

"Well?" said Miss Potts. She was shading her eyes with her hand. The sun now had complete control of the bench.

"I don't know," said Emily. "The words are the same, but the handbill I found on my desk wasn't old like this."

"*Found.*"

"Yes. I tried to tell you on the phone. I found it on my desk on the last day of classes. I don't know where it came from."

Miss Potts was blinking over in the direction of

48

the stairs. A tall, dark figure appeared to be hastening down them, coming in their direction. She rose unsteadily to her feet.

"Where is Albert?" she asked.

"He's over there, asleep, by the railing. Why, is there something wrong, Miss Potts?" She followed her gaze to the stairs. A tall man in a business suit had just stepped onto the terrace. He sat at the bench in front of Peter Pan and took a sandwich and a paperback book from his pocket. "It's just someone eating lunch," she explained to Miss Potts, who still squinted anxiously in the man's direction.

Miss Potts appeared relieved. "Perhaps we could find a little shade," she said. "If you don't mind."

"Sure. I'll just get Albert." He moaned slightly in his sleep when Emily picked him up, but he did not waken. His blond hair was slick with sweat. She laid him down in the stroller and adjusted the tattered hood to shade him from the sun. As she eased the stroller gently down the shallow steps, Miss Potts walked beside her, holding onto her arm. They walked past the patterned garden, past the topiary, down into the depths of the park. Ranks of willows lined the path, catching shadows in their leafy arms.

As they stepped into the shade, Emily felt the pressure of the thin hand on her arm ease. It perched there lightly now, like a small bird poised for flight. They walked silently for a while along the path. A slight wind whispered through the trees. From the tennis courts nearby there came the occasional flutter of applause. Finally they stopped at a bench in the shade just to the side of the path.

"And so," said Miss Potts, sighing, "the handbill is not yours. And you have no idea where it might have come from."

"No, none. It just appeared on my desk. Tell me, Miss Potts, what's this all about? What's so important about this handbill, anyway?"

"That, my dear, is a very long story. Let's just say that finding it has reminded me of something that happened a long time ago."

"Something about a magic show?"

"Yes. In fact the same magic show."

"You're kidding. You mean you were at this show. That's incredible. I've never been to a real magic show. What was it like?"

Miss Potts didn't answer right away. She took off her sunglasses and rubbed her eyes. "What was it like?" she repeated as she put them back on. "Well, to tell you the truth it was the most frightening experience of my life."

It was not the answer Emily had been expecting. She sat in stunned silence, looking at Miss Potts, who looked in turn down at the flier, her fingers restlessly flaking away the edges. When she looked up again and started speaking, a tone had entered her voice, a tone Emily had not heard before in the year she had spent in her class. She was no longer talking to her as a teacher talks to a student. It was one person to another now.

"Perhaps I should try to explain," she sighed, "though I'm afraid you might think the old lady is more than just a little crazy by the time she's done. But that, I suppose, is just the chance we'll have to take."

Chapter 9

"One summer when I was a girl a magician came to town. He gave a special children's show in the depot waiting room, and I went to it. Later that year a boy who had also been at the show died. Perhaps these were separate, totally unrelated events. Certainly no one connected the two at the time.

"I must have been about ten years old. Caledon was a very small town back then. It was the middle of the Depression. No one had much money, and nothing much happened to ease the monotony. So when one day a boy suddenly appeared on the street and pasted a flyer announcing a magic show to the pole out in front of our house, I was so excited I could hardly contain myself. I pleaded with my parents to let me go, and they finally relented.

"The show was held on a Saturday night. My father accompanied me across town to the station. It seemed the magician was staying there on a brief stopover, and the station operator had given him the use of the waiting room for the evening.

"A makeshift stage had been erected against one wall of the room. The children sat crosslegged on the floor in front of it. Many of them were unfamiliar to me and I imagined they must be farm children from the neighboring communities. I scrambled in among them beside one of the few people I recognized, Freddie Piper.

"Freddie was one of those pathetic children that seem doomed from the start. We used to call him Fat Freddie. Children can be so cruel. Nobody liked him very much. The boys considered him a sissy and refused to play with him, while the girls thought him strange. Freddie lived just down the street from us, and sometimes I took pity on him and let him play house with me.

"Freddie's response to the rejection he had suffered over the years was to bury himself in books and simply pretend you weren't there. When I sat down beside him that night, the best he could manage was a brief nod.

"My father hung around the door, along with a few of the other parents who had accompanied their children, laughing and smoking cigarettes while they waited for the show to begin. However, the magician had no sooner appeared onstage than he asked them all to leave. There were to be no adults in attendance at the children's show.

"Well, they did leave, of course, though not without some hesitation. For they must already have sensed that this was no ordinary magician.

"It is hard now to put one's finger on exactly what it was about him. It was something in the voice, the eyes. A power. Whatever it was, it lay in the air as heavily as the omnipresent odor of roses.

"The first feeling was fear, for there was in his appearance that which caused unease. His extreme pallor, the almost mechanical nature of his movements, his dark, hooded eyes. But then he spoke, and instantly the fear drifted off.

"Even now I can hear that voice: slow, melodious, each word weighed upon the tongue

52

before he let it loose. It was like listening to music. We sat there spellbound as it flowed and eddied about the room, transforming all it touched. And suddenly, it was as though we had left the world of hunger and hurt far behind and entered into another infinitely more magical realm. There was the overwhelming feeling of having long been lost and finally found one's way home. Our imaginations soared.

"Within the confines of that room, all things seemed possible—to fly, to disappear, to bring things into being with a wave of the hand. Never before had we smelled such intoxicating smells, seen such sights, heard such hauntingly beautiful words. He gathered us to him as a mother hen gathers her brood beneath her wing, and we were one.

"I felt as though I were poised on the edge of a precipice. One brief step and I would give myself over to the wonder, simply let go, and all this need never end.

"Now and then during the course of the performance the magician would call for a volunteer from the audience to come up onstage and assist him. Those who did so were rewarded with a small booklet which, the magician claimed, contained the secrets of his art. Possessing it, one shared in his power. For the first time I noticed that many of the unfamiliar children in the audience already clutched dog-eared copies of the book in their hands. They had obviously attended the show before.

"Each time the magician asked for a volunteer, arms would shoot up eagerly around the room. Beside me, Freddie would be waving his frantically. But for some reason I kept mine down.

"It may simply have been the cloying perfume of the flowers, or the incense billowing from the braziers by the stage that disordered my senses. But now and then it seemed to me that something flared briefly in those hooded eyes. I can only call it a hunger. And for an instant the magic would fail, the smile falter, and in its place I sensed the unbridled fury of a wild beast about to spring. And then it would be gone, and again there would be only the wonder.

"The show continued, and finally it came down to the last illusion, the climax of the performance. It was entitled "The Decollation of John the Baptist." The magician asked for a volunteer and again Freddie's arm shot up. Now, all night it seemed the magician had been ignoring Freddie, but this time no sooner was his arm up than the magician's eyes were on him and he nodded for him to come up. It was as if he'd been saving this for him all along.

"Freddie wove his way uncertainly through the crowd and scrambled up onto the stage. He was flushed and flustered and could barely manage to get out his name when the magician asked him.

"There was a table on the stage. The magician asked Freddie to lie down on it and shut his eyes. He covered Freddie's face with a cloth, and he asked him if he was afraid. Freddie nodded no.

"At this point the magician turned to the audience and produced a knife from his coat. It had a long curved blade and the hilt was encrusted with gems.

"He went back to the table, whispered something to Freddie, then reached beneath the cloth with the hand that held the knife. There was a quick downward thrust of his arm, a gasp from the crowd, and simultaneously a thud as the blade buried itself in the table.

"He carefully picked up the cloth and carried it

54

to the far end of the table by Freddie's feet. Setting it down gently, he turned to smile at the audience, and with a flick of his hand snatched away the cloth. There was Freddie's head.

"Someone screamed. A couple of the younger ones started wailing for their mothers. But more than a few sat there, smiling quietly to themselves.

"All of a sudden Freddie's eyes opened, and the magician began to talk to him. He asked him his name and where he was, and Freddie answered him back. I sat there awestruck, unable to believe my eyes. After a couple of minutes Freddie seemed to grow tired, and his eyes closed. The magician covered him with the cloth and carried the head back to the other end of the table, where he set it atop the motionless body. He muttered what were to us a few meaningless words. A visible tremor ran through the body, and suddenly one of Freddie's arms shot up in the air. The magician pulled off the cloth, and immediately Freddie sat up and started rubbing his eyes. The crowd went wild.

"Freddie looked around the room, confused at first. But when he realized they were clapping for him, one of his rare smiles spread across his face and he rose unsteadily to his feet. The magician thanked him for being such a good assistant, shook his hand, and gave him one of the little blue booklets. Freddie made his way off the stage and back to his seat amid the clapping of the audience.

"For the rest of the show Freddie sat there beside me in a complete daze, his eyes riveted on the magician's face, his hand clutching that flimsy little book as though his life depended on it. There was something about him, something that hadn't been there before he went up onstage.

"My eyes kept wandering to his neck. An ugly

red welt encircled it, and every now and then Freddie would reach up and absently run his fingers along it.

"Finally the show ended and we all went home. It was very late, and our parents were more than a little upset that it had gone on for so long. Some children had a hard time getting to sleep afterwards, and more than one woke up in the night, screaming. Several weary parents vowed they would confront the magician with their complaints the following day.

"Come morning, however, the magician had vanished. The room he had rented in the depot was empty, his food was untouched, and the bed showed no sign of ever having been slept in.

"Freddie was never the same after that night. Every time you saw him he had his head buried in the pages of that little book. And he was always running his hand around his neck, as though he was feeling for the seam. Before long the book was in pieces.

"He used to give magic shows in his backyard. My sister and I were usually the only ones who went. It was sad. But Freddie was convinced that he had it down to a fine art, and he would grow absolutely livid if we dared to laugh.

"Late in the fall of that year he was crossing the trestle over the ravine on the way home from school. It was a shortcut, and although it was dangerous Freddie was in a hurry to get home to practice. As usual he was reading the book.

"About midway across, he stopped suddenly, and looked back over his shoulder. He dropped the book and started to run madly for the other side. Then he jumped and plummeted off the trestle into the ravine below.

"They found him later in the bushes beneath the bridge, dead of a broken neck.

"A group of boys who had been playing in the ravine saw the whole thing. At the investigation that followed the tragedy they told of how they had seen Freddie running along the trestle, staring over his shoulder at something, before he fell. They said it looked as if he had seen a train coming.

"But there was no train.

"Separate, unrelated incidents? As I said before, no one connected the two at the time. But do you know what I think? I think that long before the fall from the bridge Freddie had already died. I think he died up there on the stage that August evening three months before.

"Maybe they had all died like that, all those strange children in the audience, that sea of blank, worshipping faces. Maybe they had all accepted the magician's invitation, had all received that flimsy little book, and had all died.

"Well, that's my story. I suppose it's obvious enough by now why I've never told anyone else before. They lock people up for less.

"And now, more than fifty years later, the handbill for that show has suddenly appeared again. Why?"

Chapter 10

More than a week went by before Craig saw Scott again. It was a week of waiting by the phone for a call that never came, of lying listlessly in front of the television for hours on end. Every fiber of his being urged him to climb on his bike and pedal over there, but he knew better. Scott had made it more than obvious that he would make the next contact. There was nothing to do but wait.

Finally, today, his mother had kicked him bodily out of the house in the interests of his health. He was in the garage now, working on his bike. The chain was full of rust. He had taken it off and was soaking it in a bucket of oil. While it soaked he washed down the frame and worked the rust from the wheel rims with steel wool. This year he would be more careful about bringing the bike indoors before the winter struck.

He dumped the rag in the bucket, dunked it up and down, and wrung it out. Although he'd opened the double doors that led onto the lane a little and the door that led from the yard, the garage was still dim. The bulb, of course, had burned out again. He might have worked in the yard on the bike, but after a week indoors the sun was just too much.

He had stationed the bike close by the door to the backyard. He told himself that this was so that he could see better, and also so that he'd be sure to hear his mother call him should the phone ring for him.

But there was another reason. There was a corner of the garage that had always made him nervous. This was the corner where the tools were stored. Garden shears, cultivators, rakes, and various other implements hung from large nails hammered into the bare studs. Among them was an old scythe with a short, stubby handle and a long, lethal-looking blade. He could not remember it ever having been taken down. When he was younger the mere sight of that scythe, its long curved blade winking dully at him from the dark, was enough to paralyze him with terror. He would imagine someone standing there in the shadows, reaching up for it. Even now he made sure he parked his bike as close to the door as possible, so he could dash out, before whatever might be waiting in that corner could get him.

As he wrung out the rag now he heard a noise from that corner, a gentle scraping, the noise the scythe might make being lifted off the nail. He glanced up, and froze. For there among the familiar shadows that inhabited the corner, there was another shadow. The rag dropped from his hands with a soft splash into the bucket.

Suddenly a flame flared in the dimness, illumining a thin, pale hand. It moved slowly through the air, settling on the end of a cigarette, illumining a lean smiling face. Scott's face.

"Hello, Craig," he said simply, blowing out the match and stepping out into the light.

Craig could feel his heart pounding crazily against his ribs, blood thundering in his head.

"How long have you been there?" was all he could say.

"Oh, for a little while." He took a drag on the cigarette. "I've been watching you work. You didn't even hear me come in."

"No."

"So how have you been keeping?"

"Not bad, I guess." The fear that had rocked his body was starting to subside now. He was able to get his breath.

"Look, why don't I give you a hand finishing up here, and maybe we can go for a ride or something."

"Yeah, all right."

It took about half an hour before the bike was cleaned up and reassembled. Scott washed up in the bucket while Craig went to tell his mother he would be going out for a while. She was delighted. Just be sure to be back in time for dinner, she told him.

"So where should we go?"

"How about my place again? I've been working on some new things."

And so it was decided. They rode double, Craig pedaling while Scott sat on the seat behind him, holding on to his waist. There were a couple of steep hills between his house and Scott's, and Craig was dreading them. He didn't want to appear weak in front of Scott, but he didn't know whether he could manage to get them both up them. Strangely enough, though, he found that he didn't have any trouble at all with the hills. The ride seemed easier, if anything, and there were times when were it not for the hands gripping his waist he would have sworn he was alone on the bike.

The blind in Scott's bedroom was drawn, as it had been before. The shade of the desk lamp had been slanted, directing a cone of light onto the floor in

60

front of the dresser. Scott had disappeared down the hall a few minutes earlier, leaving the door open a little this time. As he sat on the edge of the bed Craig listened for voices, but there was nothing. He wondered again why there never seemed to be anyone else around the place.

While he waited for Scott to get back he read the spines of the books on the shelf by the bed. *Modern Magician's Handbook, The Royal Road to Card Magic, 131 Magic Tricks*. He picked one up and thumbed through it. It was heavily underlined and annotated in the margins in a thin, spidery scrawl that didn't look like Scott's handwriting at all. Comments such as "fools" and "child's play" predominated.

Some of the books seemed very old, their ancient bindings flaking orange dust down onto the shelf. Their titles had been all but obliterated through age and handling. He slid one off the shelf and opened it to the title page. *The Discoverie of Witchcraft,* it read, by Reginald Scott. The date was printed in Roman numerals at the foot of the page: MDLXXXIV. That worked out to 1584. What on earth was a book that old doing on Scott's shelf? It belonged in a library or something. As he was returning it to its place on the shelf he noticed a small blue pamphlet that had been pushed to the rear of the shelf behind the books. The cover was crumpled and partially torn. The book had obviously been shoved to the back accidentally as another book was being returned to the shelf. He reached back into the space and brought it out.

Just then he heard the hollow sound of Scott's footsteps in the hall. Craig had meant to simply straighten out the cover of the book and return it to the shelf, but a sudden panic possessed him when he realized Scott would see him sitting there with the damaged book on his lap, no doubt believing Craig had done the damage. On a sudden impulse he shoved the book under his shirt. A second later Scott came through the door. He paused in the doorway for just an instant and Craig thought he saw his gaze settle on the shelf just briefly and the hint of a smile flit across his face.

Scott was carrying a small folding card table. He flipped down the legs and settled the table in front of the dresser in the light from the desk lamp. From under his arm he took a folded cloth and draped it over the table. It was black with gold braid around the edges and had a faintly musty smell to it.

"Now," he said, going straight into his routine, "good evening, ladies and gentlemen, boys and girls." He peered out over his imaginary audience and smiled. "Tonight you will witness the impossible. Without the aid of confederates or devices of any kind you will see sights that your eyes will not believe."

Craig sat there spellbound as Scott performed a number of tricks using cards, rope, and coins. All of them were tricks you could find in any elementary magic book. Cutting and restoring a length of rope, producing coins and making them vanish, making cards change suit or value. But he did them with a smoothness and an ease that was truly remarkable, talking all the while he was working.

He spoke of a world that had all but vanished, a world of wandering magicians with exotic sounding names and tricks, a world where objects appeared and disappeared at will, and nature was subject to the conjurer's whim. He spoke of Cagliostro, the Great Bosco, Robert-Houdin, the Hermann Brothers, discussing their styles and stage shows in such intimate detail that you could almost imagine him sitting there watching them himself.

Present-day magicians were all hacks as far as he was concerned, mere amateurs with a trunkful of gimmicks purchased from some magical supply house, and a joke or two to drag the show along. They didn't know the first thing about real magic. Real magic took years of study and practice to perform. And only the select few could unlock its secrets and seize upon its power.

He went into his Cups and Balls routine. All the while he sat there watching, Craig regretted having taken the book. He could feel it against the skin under his shirt and he was convinced each time he stood up to serve as a volunteer for one of the tricks that Scott could clearly see the bulge of it. He swore that he would find some way of getting it back on the shelf before he left.

But he didn't. Scott never let him out of his sight from that point on, it seemed. And suddenly at four thirty he packed up his things and asked Craig to leave. There was someplace he had to go, he said. Something he had to do. As they were saying goodbye Craig swore that Scott could see right through his shirt to the stolen book. He felt sick with fear and dread.

"Scott," he said, as he was turning to go.

"Yes?" Scott was standing in front of the mirror, combing his hair.

And he almost managed to get the confession out. Almost, but something in Scott's eyes stopped him, stopped him dead. And all he said was, "Ah, nothing. I was just wondering when we'd get together again."

"Soon. Very soon."

"Yeah."

All the way home that "Very soon" kept sounding in his head. It was as though there was a sinister threat beneath the words. Or was it only his own anxiety screaming back at him?

Right after dinner that night he went upstairs, locked the door and took the book down from where he had hidden it at the back of his closet. He experienced an initial surge of panic when he couldn't find it, and had worked himself into quite a state, throwing the stuff that was piled up there onto the floor of the closet, before his hand settled on the thin blue paper of the pamphlet where it had fallen to the back of the shelf.

He went and lay across his bed with the book. The pamphlet was entitled *Secrets of the Magick Art*. The author was not named. All it contained were about a dozen simple sleights of hand involving cards and coins. Each of them was crudely illustrated with closeups of hands detailing the mechanics of the illusion.

It might simply have been his frame of mind but the mere sight of the drawings unnerved Craig to such a degree that he finally had to close the book. The primitive, sticklike hands clutching the coins seemed strangely menacing. They were like the fleshless hands of a skeleton.

That night his dreams were full of magic. Coins appeared and disappeared in the air. Skeletal hands shuffled cards with lightning speed, tossing them into the air where they became huge black birds, their wings beating thunderously in the air. At one point he woke up, his head full of the sound, only to find a strong wind battering the window shade against the frame. He climbed out of bed and closed the window.

It took him a long time to get back to sleep. He

kept staring over at the closet where the book was hidden, every nerve in his body on edge. Twice he thought he heard the light chime of empty hangers knocking against one another in there. But he would not have left his bed to open that door for the world.

First thing the next morning he got the book down, tucked it under his shirt, and pedaled back to Scott's place. There was no one there.

Chapter 11

August in the Endicott household usually meant two weeks in the wilds of Lake Scugogg at the cottage mother had inherited from her family. There was only one problem with the cottage—it was smaller than the house. This meant that if the weather was against you you stood a good chance of going insane by the second day of the trip. If the weather was good you might last a week if you were lucky.

The rooms were divided by half walls. This afforded about the same degree of privacy as holding a paper towel in front of your face. Albert hadn't liked the cottage at all last year. You could tell, because he spent most of his time screaming. When he periodically passed out from exhaustion, the rest of the family was left tiptoeing around the place doing shallow breathing in case they woke him up.

Bedtime at the cottage came early. By nine o'clock everyone was cross-eyed from looking for puzzle pieces by the light of the kerosene lamp and exhausted from that day's expedition to the beach. The beach seemed to be situated about halfway between the cottage and the city. By the time you reached the water you were too tired to swim, so you just lay in the sand and screamed while the flies ate you alive.

No one was exactly brokenhearted when Mr. Endicott announced that they would not be going to the cottage this summer since he would be tied up for most of August with work for the historical society. In addition to the cleanup of the depot, there was the scale model he was working on in the garage. It was to be the centerpiece of the museum, a duplication of the depot and the main features of the town earlier in the century. Finally it seemed as though father's trains were going to find a permanent home.

It was Saturday afternoon. A week had gone by since Emily's meeting with Miss Potts in the park. She had heard nothing further during that time. The whole thing was just too fantastic. Her natural inclination was to cast it all aside as simply one more of Miss Potts's eccentricities, which were many. They included stopping suddenly in the middle of a sentence in class and staring off into space, talking to her plants, and eating her hair.

Basically, the woman was weird. But something in the tone of her voice as she had told that incredible story, something in the frail, trusting touch of her hand as they had walked down into the park, stopped her from dismissing it all.

Emily pushed the stroller down the shady side of the street. Albert, lulled by the rhythmic rattle of the wheels crossing the cracks in the pavement, had passed out about five minutes ago. His head was dangling over the side of the stroller. An old lady who had just gone by had almost taken off the top of it with her bundle buggy. At the risk of waking him, Emily decided to chance rearranging him. She flipped the backrest down to the prone position and gently urged him off the side of the stroller.

Instantly his eyes snapped open. He briefly

considered screaming, then promptly passed out again. She flipped the brim of his bonnet down over his eyes and quickly started pushing the stroller again. Within two minutes he was snoring like an old drunk.

Mother was not coping at all well today. Charles had thrown up twice in the night and hadn't made it to the toilet either time. In fact he hadn't made it out of the bed. Charles was rather difficult to deal with when he was sick. He lay bug-eyed in the bed, paralyzed at the prospect of what might be about to happen, and convinced that if he just lay there perfectly still and stopped breathing everything would be all right. Consequently, when the inevitable finally occurred, Charles was still lying there.

Emily had been awakened both times. The first time to the sound of soiled laundry being thrown down the stairs, the second to mother's shrill warning that if he did it again he'd sleep in it for the rest of the night.

This morning Charles had staged a miraculous recovery. He had been fit enough in fact to bash Elizabeth over the head with the Viewmaster when she wouldn't surrender the slides she was sitting on.

That had awakened mother. You could tell just by the way she folded the bed back into the couch that it was going to be a bad day. By the end of breakfast her eyes still weren't open.

Albert, still too young to read the situation and shut his mouth, had decided to stage a temper tantrum shortly after mother started the laundry. Emily had emerged from her room just in time to see mother coming for him with murder written all over her face. It was then Emily suggested that she take Albert with her to the library.

He was still snoring into the brim of his bonnet

68

when they arrived. Emily parked the stroller in the shade by the building and went in. Five minutes later she reemerged with an armload of murder mysteries snatched at random from the rack. Mother devoured one of these at a sitting, then ran around the house checking all the doors and windows. It was her idea of light reading.

Albert started to stir when Emily wedged the books in beside him. By the time they reached the traffic lights at the corner he was already into the initial stages of back-arching, his face flushed from battling the plastic strap. In about ten seconds he would rediscover his voice. And use it. Well rested, Albert was ready again to loose himself upon the world.

They were halfway down the block when the first scream broke.

"Out!" screamed Albert. "Out!" The trouble with letting Albert out was that he didn't draw much distinction between the sidewalk and the street. Given half the chance, he would run right off the curb into the traffic, if only because he knew Emily didn't want him to. And even if she could manage to coax him away from the curb, he would toddle up every walk they came to on the way home. There were a lot of walks between the library and their house. They might make it back by tomorrow morning—if Albert hurried.

She let him scream and flail, pretending not to know him.

" 'Keem! Keem!' " wailed Albert as soon as he saw the variety store on the corner.

"Okay, Albert. If Emily gets you keem will you be a good boy and stay in the stroller?"

He bobbed his blond head enthusiastically.

"All right. But one peep out of you, Albert, just

69

one peep and I'll eat all the keem myself. Understand? Now you just sit here and be good. I'll be back in a minute."

It took a little longer than a minute. By the time she got back the books were lying face-down on the sidewalk and Albert was busy watching the library cards blow down the street.

"Keem!" he yelled when he saw her coming. "Keem!"

It was keem, all right. Chocolate keem, the only kind they had left. It was already beginning to melt. Emily licked the soft brown mush and sent Albert into hysterics.

"Okay, okay. I just don't want it dripping all over everything. For crying out loud, Albert, will you shut up before I paint your face with it?"

She handed him the cone, picked up the books, and went to retrieve the cards. By the time she got back Albert was already doing a pretty good job of painting his face himself.

He'd take one loving lick, hold it at arm's length and watch it melt for a couple of minutes, then take another. It broke his heart to have to eat it, so he kept taking smaller licks and longer pauses. By the time they were halfway home the keem was liquid and the cone was limp. Albert clutched it in his hands like a pastry bag.

Emily had tried licking it around the edges for a while to keep it from getting all over the place, but after about two blocks the cone looked so disgusting that she couldn't stomach it anymore, much less listen to Albert's screaming. His face was chocolate, his hands were chocolate, his clothes were chocolate. The seat of the stroller was puddled in goo, and the library books, which she had rescued too late, were glued together.

70

She couldn't bring him back home looking like this. Mother would kill her. She was still trying to get the popsicle stains out of his sunsuit from that day on the porch. Emily began looking for a place where she could park the stroller and clean him up a little.

Since the library was on the west side of town, to get back home they would have to go right past the depot. Mr. Endicott had said that he would be spending some time there today, so Emily decided to take the side street closest to the station and see whether he was still there. She turned onto Bedford Road and crossed the bridge over the ravine. Just on the other side of the bridge lay the strip of railway land that cut through town, a sea of ragweed and witchgrass. The old track ran right through the center of the strip. Where it passed over the road there was a level crossing and a set of warning lights that someone had used for target practice. It didn't work anymore, but didn't really have to for all the rail traffic that Caledon saw these days.

In the distance she could see the depot, perched on the edge of the ravine. There was no sign of the car. Dad had probably already been and gone. It looked as if someone had been tidying up the grounds around the building. The grass had been scythed down and bundled and a stack of garbage was piled against the side of the depot. Still, it was hard to see how the old ruin could ever be brought back to life.

This was as good a place as any to change Albert. She wheeled the stroller off the sidewalk and into the field, following a path that was far too narrow for it. It didn't take too long before the grass and weeds had wrapped around the wheels and she had to stop.

She lay Albert down in the grass on top of one of the spare diapers from the bag attached to the back of the stroller and started peeling off his chocolate clothes. There was no sign of the damp cloth mother usually packed into the bag, so she settled for a clean diaper, moistening a corner of it with her mouth and trying to clean up Albert as well as she could. There was a definite odor coming off him that was more than chocolate keem. He had that pensive look he got when he was sitting in it.

"Oh no, Albert, you didn't." She peeked down the back of his pants. He had. She toyed briefly with the idea of letting him wear it for the rest of the way home and decided she couldn't stand the thought of it. Holding her breath, she unpinned the diaper. Actually it wasn't as bad as it might have been. And when she was finished Albert looked a lot less pensive. He started running through the grass, catching at it with open arms, squealing with delight as it tickled his face.

It was as she was bundling the dirty things back into the bag that she first heard the noise from over in the direction of the depot. It was an odd noise, and for a moment she was unable to place it. It sounded almost like a burst of muffled applause at first, or like a flock of birds taking flight. But there were no birds.

Albert had heard the noise as well and immediately scurried off down the path to investigate. By the time Emily noticed him he was already at the depot, hoisting his leg up onto the platform.

"Albert, come back here," she called, running after him, leaving their things lying there in the grass. She lost sight of him as he disappeared behind the pile of garbage lying on the platform.

As she raced across the rough stubble of the

newly cut grass she heard the sound again. It had a strange quality to it—hollow, distant. It seemed to be coming from everywhere and nowhere at once. This time something like a squeal was woven in with it. Or was it the cry of a bird?

The lock and chain that secured the door of the depot were lying on platform. The door stood open. A sharp, musty smell drifted out. The odor of dampness, laced with decay.

"Albert?" she called into the shadows, and heard a flurry of footsteps inside. "Albert, you come out of there this instant." Something like fear was starting to raise its nasty head inside her. Why was the door open? What had that noise been?

She walked through the open door and into a dim hallway. Midway along the wall on her left there was a window with an ornamented iron grill over it. A ticket window. Beneath it on the floor lay a drop sheet, and on the drop sheet, cans of unopened paint, brushes, and paint trays. She recognized a mop and pail as having come from home. The sight of the familiar objects helped allay her fears.

At the far end of the opposite wall there was a doorway. She could hear someone moving around in there. Albert. She stepped cautiously through the doorway and found herself in the depot's large circular waiting room. The floor was filled with rubble. Broken benches, piles of yellowed newspapers. In one spot the ceiling had come through. Someone had swept the fallen plaster into a pile.

"So there you are," she said. Albert was standing stock still on the far side of the room, at the foot of a winding metal staircase. "Emmy's very angry with you," she warned, crossing the room to get him. He was holding something in one of his hands. He must

73

have found it on the floor. It looked like a flower petal.

She took him by the shoulders. "That was bad, Albert, running away like that." His lip quivered and he looked like he was going to cry. He swung his head around, straining to look up the stairs.

"What is it, Albert?" she asked nervously, and in the same instant heard the slight creak of a floorboard overhead. Her eyes darted to the top of the stairs. With a sudden and overwhelming certainty she knew that someone was standing up there, just out of sight.

Pure panic swept over her, and for instant she was paralyzed. Then in a single motion she caught Albert up in her arms and raced for the door. She did not stop running until the stroller abruptly loomed up in her path.

She hastily threw their scattered belongings into it and dragged it along behind them, its clogged wheels bumping crazily along the path. It was not until she felt the concrete of the sidewalk underfoot that she stopped and let herself look back. No one was there.

That night over dinner she mentioned to dad as casually as she could manage that she'd passed by the depot earlier in the day, looking for him, and had noticed that the lock was off the door. She failed to add that she had actually been in the place and nearly been frightened out of her mind. Albert's excited babble about "the 'tairs" and "the dark" met with polite disregard.

Mr. Endicott explained that he had left early. One of the other men must have forgotten to lock up. He would look into it later. But perhaps in future it might be wiser if she steered clear of the depot. It was not the sort of place a young girl should be hanging about, as isolated and wild as the area was.

"'Cared," said Albert. "'Cared." And mother commented on how much he was talking tonight. But no one knew he was trying to tell them he'd been scared. No one but Emily.

Chapter 12

The Children's Show

II

The magician walked to the rear of the stage, returning with an artist's portfolio, which he set upon a small trestle in front of the table. The portfolio was about three feet long by two feet wide, with a thickness of about two inches, the sort of thing one sees art students carrying their work around in. It was positioned in such a way that when it was opened he was able to reach into it and yet the audience was unable to see inside.

He began to produce a number of sketches from the portfolio. One of a candelabrum, another of a vase of flowers, a third of a pair of pigeons, and so on. There were well over a dozen of them altogether. Having set them aside, he returned to the portfolio and began, astonishingly, to draw from it the very items depicted in the sketches, laying them one by one on the table. In no time at all the table was completely covered with the articles, all of which had come, incredibly, from the narrow confines of the portfolio. The children's mouths hung open in amazement.

Peering yet again into the depths of the portfolio,

the magician's hand now emerged with a small potted orange tree. He set it down on the edge of the stage, where in full view of the audience it began miraculously to bloom and bear fruit. He plucked the oranges from the tree and passed them out to the children at the foot of the stage.

"Taste," he said. They did, and found that the fruit was real.

Amidst the delighted applause of the assembled, the magician took his bow. Suddenly, however, he straightened, and turning toward the portfolio, cocked his head to one side, listening.

"Did any of you hear anything just then?" he asked. In the sudden stillness the children strained to hear.

The magician walked, almost cautiously, back to the portfolio and leaned down over it. "Yes," he said, "I do believe there is still something else here, tucked away back in the corner."

He reached his whole arm in now, bending far down into the portfolio, as if he were feeling around some vast inner space. "Aha!" came a muffled and victorious voice at last. "There we are."

This time when he emerged he appeared to be clutching a matted fur coat in his hand. He smelled it tentatively, wrinkling up his nose at it, and dropped it in a heap on the stage.

As it landed, however, an incredible thing occurred. For an instant the fur seemed to tremble. Then it suddenly bumped itself up in the center, and four thin gray limbs appeared, holding it aloft. A bushy tail swept down to the floor. A dog, thought the children in astonishment.

And then, with a horrific growl, the creature whirled to face them. It was a huge gray wolf, its eyes red with rage. When it saw the children there, it leaped to the edge of the stage, snarling, and perched there as though about to pounce.

Several children began shrieking hysterically, while others raced frantically for the door. The wolf darted from one end of the stage to the other, growling wildly and baring its long yellow fangs, incensed by their cries. Meanwhile, the magician stood back calmly against the curtain and watched, a look of terrifying delight etched on his face.

At last the wolf grew so enraged that with one terrific bound it sprang from the stage into the air. Just before it fell upon one cowering child in the first row, the magician lightly clapped his hands. For an instant the wolf appeared to hover in midair. There was a muffled explosion and a sudden flash like a fireworks display, and a shower of rose petals scattered down over the children. The wolf was gone.

"Reality or illusion?" asked the magician, as he closed the portfolio and slid it to the rear of the stage. "Which is which?"

Chapter 13

For the past half hour Mr. Palmer had been busy overhead endlessly repeating the opening bars of Telemann's Suite in A Minor on his recorder. It was beginning to irk her just slightly. Nightly, for at least forty-five minutes before he went to bed, Mr. Palmer practiced. It was a wonder to her that he was able to sleep afterwards.

Miss Potts sat on the window seat, her shawl about her shoulders against the night air. On her lap lay a tin of English biscuits that one of her students had presented to her on the last day of classes. For the past three weeks it had sat untouched on her closet shelf, but now she was picking idly through it, ferreting out her favorites, the ones wrapped in red foil. She always ate when she was feeling edgy or nervous, and she was more nervous now than she had ever been in her life.

Try though she might, she could not get the handbill out of her mind. It occupied her thoughts from morning till night. And even then there was no escape, for all night long she did nothing but dream of the Children's Show.

Now she could call up every detail of that evening's performance. She would sit for hours in her room as if in a trance, reading repeatedly through the playbill, recalling with alarming clarity each illusion, down to the very words the magician had spoken at the time. She was unable to stop herself.

Finally, last night she had caught sight of herself in the mirror and been so shocked by what she saw that she immediately took action. There was an old wooden wardrobe in one corner of her room, on top of which she stored, among other things, her old photo albums. She had forced herself to fold up the handbill and had tucked it away between the pages of the top album on the pile. For the first time in over a week her sleep had been peaceful and undisturbed by dreams.

This morning, in fact, she had felt relaxed enough to resume her cleaning of the classroom. She finished quickly with the desks and moved on to the supply closet. Here there were papers to sift through, sort, and stack in orderly piles upon the shelves, all tasks guaranteed to anchor one's mind firmly in the mundane and keep the mysterious at bay.

More than once, however, while she was working, she had caught herself suddenly staring toward the back of the classroom with the strange feeling that someone else had entered the room. For some reason her eyes kept settling on the desk that the new boy had occupied. She would not have been surprised to see Scott Renshaw sitting there, staring back at her and smiling that unnerving smile of his. She left after little more than an hour, leaving a note on the door asking Mr. Murphy to water her plants if he had the time.

The recorder showed signs of failing upstairs. Balls of red foil littered the window seat and her lap was covered in crumbs. She clapped the lid down on the tin, brushed the crumbs off into the wastebasket. Again her eyes wandered to the wall above her desk where the bank calendar hung. After dinner she had been fussing about the desk, busying herself in an effort to keep herself from reaching up for the photo album. She noticed that she had not yet turned the page on the calendar to August, which had begun yesterday.

The calendar came compliments of the Greater Niagara Trust Company, where she banked. The top half of the calendar was a photograph that changed from month to month. The bottom half showed the numbered grid of days and dates for the month. August's picture was of two puffins with brightly colored bills, sitting on a rock romancing.

It was not the photo that caught her attention now, however. It was something she had noticed when she flipped the page. Because the show had been so much on her mind, the eighth of the month seemed to almost leap off the page at her. For that had been the date of the show, August 8, 1936. What struck her as curious, however, was that the eighth this year fell on a Saturday, as it had then.

For some reason this coincidence caused an indefinable dread to swell in the pit of her stomach. She scolded herself for such unreasonable alarm. After all, how many August eighths between 1936 and now must have fallen on a Saturday? Several, no doubt. And besides, what was she thinking anyway?

She returned the tin of cookies to her closet and crossed the room to shut the drapes for the night. While doing so she happened to notice something out the window. She stopped in her tracks, staring out at the silhouette of the depot against the night sky. For an instant it looked as if there had been a light on in there. She reached over and turned off the reading lamp and stood there silently in the dark, watching. There was nothing now. Nothing but her imagination working overtime. She caught the corner of the drape in her hand and was about to guide it behind the window seat when she saw the light again. There was no mistaking it this time. Someone was in the depot.

What it was that prompted her to immediately fetch her sweater from the closet and quietly open her door she probably could not have said. Now was not the time for thought. She peeked her head out into the hall. Mrs. Holmes's door was closed. She tiptoed quietly down the stairs, keeping to the edge, where they were least likely to creak. Miss Blight would be back in her room watching the television. The lights in the two front rooms were off. There was only the dim yellow glow from the Tiffany lamp in the hall.

The front door was bolted for the night. Miss Potts quietly slid the chain off and undid the latch. In an instant she was out on the porch, heart pounding, wondering what on earth she was up to. There was an old broom propped against the wall. She took it with her.

As she crept along the alleyway at the side of the house she could hear the TV on in Miss Blight's room. She cautiously crept past the partially open window, feeling her way along the wall. Near the back of the house she tripped over the dark coil of garden hose on the ground. The miniature poodle next door emerged from its hole under the porch and began to bark.

"Shhh, Samantha. It's only me. You be quiet now, or there'll be no more treats for you," she warned.

Whether it was the threat or simply the sound of

the familiar voice, Samantha retired to her hole, delivered two sharp petulant barks to the dark, and was still.

The moon was on the rise and the garden was washed in silver. Mr. Palmer had applied a fresh coat of white paint to the lawn furniture earlier in the week. It sat in a somehow eerie circle by the rose trellis.

The damp grass had soaked through her canvas shoes before she was halfway to the gate at the rear of the garden. Shadows, gathered in the shade of the poplars, crept out to observe the intruder. The sight of a darker shape under one of the trees startled Miss Potts more than she wished to admit. And when the shape resolved itself into the stepladder Mr. Palmer had been using to trim dead branches from the tree, she was not as relieved as she should have been. Here, in the stillness of the night garden, it was no longer the paint-splattered ladder that stood at the foot of the basement stairs. Now it was an instrument of the night. She imagined pale, lean figures leaping down from the tree onto it, scrambling off into the garden.

She gave the ladder a wide berth and held the sweater close about her, as if it were armor, able to protect her.

She closed the back gate behind her and started across the field between herself and the depot. The tall grass seemed to grab for her bare legs, as if to hold her back. Burrs caught at the hem of her dress. The crickets suddenly were still. She longed for the safety of her room, the open tin of biscuits on her lap, Mr. Palmer's slippered feet creaking the floor-boards overhead.

It was as she scrambled up the roadbed and onto the tracks that the first wave of unreasoned fear engulfed her. The roadbed had hidden the depot from her before. Now she again saw the light through the shuttered window. It looked now like someone peeking through lowered eyelids, pretending to be asleep.

Suddenly the depot itself seemed sinister to her. She had the strange feeling that it was laughing at her, standing there dwarfed by the night, presuming to pit herself against it. For a moment she saw the magician's face superimposed over the dark outline. She stumbled over the rail and went tumbling head over heels down the grading and into the weedy gully.

She brushed herself off and glanced up again. The illusion was gone. There was only the depot. She saw now that the front door was slightly ajar. Shaken slightly by the fall, she pushed on unsteadily toward the platform.

As she mounted the stairs and edged her way toward the door she remembered Fat Freddie walking up the stairs to the stage where the Professor waited.

Inside the building now she heard something. The low hollow lilt of someone whistling.

Chapter 14

Emily knocked on the garage door again. It was late afternoon and there was a delicious calm about the backyard. In the corner by the laundry stoop stood a pile of grass cuttings, the rake protruding from it. The mower had been abandoned in the middle of the lawn, looking like some strange beast grazing. The scene bore the unmistakable stamp of father's handiwork—close to, but not quite, complete.

Mr. Endicott was a mass of half-completed projects and elaborate plans. When the family had first moved into the bungalow, it had been with visions of adding another room onto the back of the house, digging out the basement and putting a family room down there, and several other variations on the theme. He still had all the plans filed away in the cabinet by the workbench. Now and then when the house seemed about to burst from the strain of the six of them, he would take out the plans and pore over them for a day or two. But nothing ever came of it, because Mr. Endicott would never consider anyone but himself doing it, and doing it was the part he liked least.

The ice tinkled delicately against the side of the glass Emily was carrying. Lemonade, meant to lure dad back to the job. She rapped on the door again, this time pressing her ear to the wood. She could hear the muffled din of machinery inside.

Behind her a screen door slammed. She glanced over her shoulder in time to see Walter, who lived next door, swaggering down his porch steps. He was dressed to the teeth for his date. Mechanic's coveralls undone practically down to his navel, just in case the world was in any doubt as to exactly how many hairs he had on his chest, an oily rag billowing from his back pocket. In one hand he clutched a set of socket wrenches like a bouquet of flowers for his Baby. Baby was up on blocks in the clapboard and sheet-metal monstrosity they called their garage.

"Hey, dollface," he called. "Gonna come and cut mine next?" He bobbed his head in the direction of the mower and cracked a little smile that somehow managed to carry a leer along with it.

The yard he was now walking through was straight out of the jungle. The grass, grown hip high and gone to seed, was crushed down in one wide swath from the stoop to the garage. Somewhere beneath the riot of green lay the rusted corpses of a motorbike, a go-cart, and several dismembered bicycles. Former loves. If he ever broke up with Baby they were going to need a bigger backyard.

"No, I don't think so, Walter. It might die of the shock." Emily could remember back to when Walter was the weird kid who used to patrol the lane, smelling gas tanks. The first phase in a lifelong infatuation for anything with wheels. It had probably fried his brain.

Emily knew Walter hated to be called Walter. Since Baby had arrived on the scene, the name had been "Rocky." The only thing rocky about Walter was the inside of his head.

86

He stopped dead in his tracks when he heard the hated name. For an instant you could see him considering jumping the joke of a fence that separated the yards, and trying out his socket wrenches on her. Instead, he smiled.

"Quite a sense of humor you've got there, kid. You should be on TV or something." He disappeared through the door of the garage, slamming it behind him. It trembled a little, as if it wanted to fall down. Emily saw the light go on through the cracks in the slats and heard the metal echo of the lovers' embrace.

Dad still hadn't answered. She set the lemonade down on the grass and walked around to the side of the garage, over the heaved flagstones of the patio that had never quite been finished, past the barbeque that doubled as a birdbath. She climbed up onto the inverted oil drum that would make a great garbage can just as soon as dad got around to painting it. Cupping her hands to her face, she squinted in through the grimy window.

It was hard to see much of anything. All she could make out was the twisted blur of track coiled like a sleeping dragon in the center of the murky room, and looming over it a barely human-looking blob that was most likely her father.

Her sharp rap on the glass sheared a spider's web. The spider drifted down to investigate. Spiders came a close second to centipedes on her top ten list of terrors. She screamed and sprang back from the window. The oil drum teetered briefly, then fell on its side with a terrific crash.

Simultaneously two doors opened. From one of them emerged Walter, already up to his elbows in grease, from the other, Mr. Endicott, blinking against the light. He knocked the lemonade over onto the grass.

"Hey, are you all right?" asked Walter, dangling his arms over the fence.

"Yeah, I'm okay." It was a brave lie. She had twisted her ankle, and waves of pain were shooting up her leg.

Father was at her side now, helping her to her feet. As she put weight on the leg she winced.

"You've hurt yourself."

"Just twisted my ankle. It's nothing, really."

The clatter of the model trains could be heard through the open garage door. Walter, who had no idea what went on in there, cocked his head to one side and looked confused.

"Say, what's that?" he said. He worked his way along the fence, trying to get a peek through the open door. "Watcha doin' in there, Mr. Endicott?"

Father was helping Emily to the garage, doing his best to ignore Walter. The less the neighbors knew about the valuable collection housed in the garage, the better he felt about it.

"Sounds like trains," said Walter. He looked awfully stupid when he was confused.

"Walter, will you please pipe down? Can't you see I'm in pain?"

Dad helped Emily in through the door and sat her down in a chair. He returned to shut the door. "Thank you very much for your concern, Walter," he said, hugging the door close to his head. "I think we'll be all right now."

"Yeah, but—" The door shut.

"Sure sounded like trains," said Walter as he cut a new swath through the grass on his way back to Baby.

"Now," said father, "let's take a look at that

ankle.'' He felt gingerly around the bone, while Emily gritted her teeth and tried not to scream.

"I think you'll live," he announced. "Just a sprain. What on earth were you doing on top of that oil drum anyway?''

"I was knocking at the window trying to get your attention. I couldn't get an answer at the door. Mother sent me out with some lemonade for you. She was wondering about the lawn.''

"Oh yes, the lawn. That's what I came in for in the first place. The mower needs oiling. I must have gotten sidetracked.'' He went to the control panel and pulled the switches, cutting the power to the track. The trains ground to a halt. In the sudden silence Emily realized she'd been shouting over the noise.

The gardening tools were hung on nails on the wall of the garage. Dad reached up, took down the shears, and decided they could use a drop of oil. He started rooting through his stuff for the oil can.

Emily admired the layout. It had grown considerably since her father had moved it out of the house. Now it occupied the better part of the garage. In the center of the layout stood a scale model of the Caledon Depot earlier in the century. With its gleaming copper cornice and the elaborate gingerbread ornamentation throughout, it looked like something out of a fairy tale. It was painted white with deep green trim around the window hoods and in the angles of the gables. She found herself staring intently at it, picturing Miss Potts as a girl walking through that narrow door with the pink pebbleglass sidelights on her way to a magic show. A slight shiver ran up her spine as she remembered what had happened to her there yesterday with Albert.

"Ah, here it is.'' Mr. Endicott had unearthed the

oil can on a table littered with shredded sponge and twigs from the lilac bush, the makings for the trees in the layout. He noticed Emily admiring the depot.

"Like it?" he asked.

"Yes," she said. "It's beautiful."

"Oh, that reminds me. I dropped by there last evening after you'd gone to bed. Just to check up on the place, you know. She was locked up as tight as a drum. I decided to take a quick look around anyway while I was there. I came across something quite interesting, actually. A handbill of some sort. It was posted on the wall of the waiting room. I thought we'd cleared all that stuff away last week and I was a little surprised to see it there. I think I have it here somewhere."

He started rummaging through his pockets. "Anyway," he continued, "I nearly got the fright of my life. I was sitting there giving it a look over and I heard a noise behind me in the hall. I turned around and there was this old woman standing in the doorway, staring at me. It gave me quite a turn, I'll tell you. When I found my voice I asked her if I could help her. I realized by that point that she was far more frightened than I was.

"She just mumbled something about having made a mistake and thinking I was someone else and then she wandered off. I saw her crossing the field and going into one of those yards that face the depot. She was a strange one, I'll tell you. Who did she expect to find over here at that time of night? Well, it takes all kinds to make a world, as my mother used to say, God rest her soul.

"Ah, here it is." He had been through every pocket twice while he told the tale. Now, in the inner pocket of his vest he had found what he'd been looking for.

90

"There," he said, as he spread the crumpled yellow paper out on his worktable. "Now just take a look at this, will you?"

Peering over his shoulder in the dim light of the garage, Emily found herself staring down at another flier for the Children's Show.

Chapter 15

The seat of Craig's pants was wet from sitting on the damp boards of the breezeway, and when he stood up now his knees cracked. Twice in the time he'd been there he'd heard the echo of footsteps on the fire escape, each time expecting it was Scott returning home. The first time it had been the young mother who lived across the way, carrying her little boy, his blond head lolling in the crook of her arm. The second time, when he was sure it was Scott at last, a huge man with pale pink and green tattoos covering both arms had appeared at the top of the stairs. He had stopped when he saw Craig sitting there, eyed him silently for a few seconds, then shuffled past. The boards of the breezeway groaned beneath his weight. He disappeared through the door at the far end, and a minute later there was a faint flutter of curtains in a window as he peered out. There was something in the look that Craig didn't like, a sort of sleepy violence.

He glanced down at his watch again. It was well after five. His mother would be going mad with worry, but he couldn't leave yet. He leaned over the railing and looked down the lane. At the rear of the restaurant a dog was rooting through a bag of garbage. Close by a car door slammed. The dog jumped, then watched warily as the car pulled away from its parking spot and bumped off down the rutted lane.

There was no sign of Scott anywhere. Again Craig checked his back pocket for the book, then turned and slowly descended the stairs. He waited there for half an hour more, sitting on the seat of the bike. It still gleamed from the cleaning he and Scott had given it three days ago. They had been three of the longest days of his life.

He had finally moved the book out of the house last night, afraid of spending another night alone with it in his room. He had wrapped it in a clean chamois and hidden it in the rafters of the garage. Still, those hands had haunted his sleep and twice in the night he had awakened to the garage door rattling in the wind.

But far worse than the fear of the book, worse even than his fear of Scott's anger at his having taken it, was the mounting fear that he might not see Scott again. He couldn't have stood that. There was a constant ache inside him now, as if some vital part of him had been torn out. He suddenly realized just how much of himself ·he had given over to Scott. And in return Scott had offered him—what? The sudden promise of power where before there had only been fear. A tantalizing glimpse of a world where magic held sway.

By now a night smell had started to creep out from the gardens across the way, the damp green smell of growing things. The lane was filling up with shadows. He decided to leave.

As he turned onto Arlington with the bike, an idea hit him. Why didn't he try the front door to Scott's place? Maybe there was someone home after all and they just hadn't heard him banging at the back when he first came. It was worth a try. Anything was better than heading back home with the book.

The problem was that he had never been to Scott's by the front way, and as he slowly drove along the street, dodging sewer gratings, he quickly realized that without an address he'd never find the place. Shop after shop lined the street, each one with a door beside it leading to the apartments above. And they all looked the same. He had just about given up and decided to go home, when one of those doors opened and the tattooed man emerged, disappearing into a cigar store two doors down.

That was the place. It had to be. All three apartments must share the same entranceway. He got off the bike, peered cautiously into the store and saw the fat man fanning through a magazine. He leaned the bike against a lamp post and hurried for the door.

The store beside the apartment entrance was a beauty salon. Mannikin heads were lined up in the window wearing pastel-colored wigs. A sign reading No Appointment Necessary hung in the door.

The trapped stale smell of heat and dirt leaped out at him as he edged open the apartment door and went in. The floor at the foot of the stairs that led up to the second floor landing was littered with handbills and garbage blown in off the street. The name slots in the battered metal mail boxes were empty. He started up the stairs.

The hall light wasn't working, but in the shadows he could see a pile of newspapers stacked outside the door nearest to him. Further down the hall a carriage sat outside a second door. Past that, facing him from the far end of the hall, there was a third door. Instinctively he headed for that door.

As he approached it he saw that the door was

94

covered in crayon scrawl and dirty fingerprints. A frayed rush mat lay on the floor in front of it. Standing there in the dim hall he felt suddenly afraid.

He knocked on the door. The sound seemed to echo through the apartment beyond like a penny dropped down a sewer pipe.

He should have turned and left right then. He knew he should have. Instead he went down on one knee and pressed his eye to the keyhole, straining to make something of the bright blur of light on the other side. It was like staring into the heart of a fire. Suddenly the handle was hot. There was a smell of smoke in the air.

"Hey, what are you doing there?"

The voice hit him in the small of the back like a sledgehammer. Ice raced up his spine. He sprang away from the door and whirled to see a massive shadow blocking the head of the stairs.

"I said, what the hell do you think you're doing there?" The fat man had dropped the parcel he was carrying to the floor. He squeezed sideways past the carriage.

"I'm not doing anything, mister. Honest. I was just looking for my friend."

"Your friend my ass, you little punk. Your friend don't live there."

"Yes he does, mister. I swear." But doubt had already entered his voice. He edged back against the door. The handle was cold against his arm. The only smell in the air now was that of his own fear.

"I oughta break your arm, you little creep. I seen you sneakin' around here. You're the one was at my window the other night, aren't you?"

The man was arched over him now like a giant. The shadows hid his face, a heavy rancid odor

95

poured off him. As the huge tattooed arm scooped to grab him, Craig squirmed free. He bounced off the carriage, sending it slamming into the door.

"Look, mister," he screamed, "you're crazy! I was just looking for my friend. He lives there."

The man was enraged now. He growled as he pushed past the carriage in pursuit. Craig took off down the stairs, stumbling over the package the man had dropped at the top, saving himself by catching hold of the railing. It shook beneath his weight, and as if in slow motion, he watched the bread that was in the bag pop loose and go bouncing down the stairs ahead of him, the soft white slices scattering over the dirty tiles.

He was halfway down the block, pedaling furiously, before the fat man stormed onto the street, screaming after him, dirty slices of bread clutched to his chest.

Chapter 16

The following afternoon Emily made her way across town to try and find Miss Potts. Her search through the phone book that morning had proven futile. There was no entry under the name. All she really had to go on now was the fact that Miss Potts had mentioned that she could see the depot from her room. That, and father's story of the old woman who had surprised him last night. There was no doubt in Emily's mind who that woman had been.

Father said she had disappeared into one of the yards opposite the depot. There was only one street whose yards overlooked the depot, Vintner Avenue, a street that followed the course of the tracks straight through town. When the Endicott clan went for their Sunday afternoon drive, it was almost certain that at some point they would turn onto Vintner so that father could catch sight of the station and the old wooden trestle that bridged the ravine.

Emily could vaguely recall sitting on father's lap in the car when she was very young, parked on a dirt turnoff from Vintner, waiting for the train to pass and the conductor to wave and blow the whistle. It was subject to debate who got the bigger thrill from the experience, father or herself. Now, of course, that was a thing of the past. Emily could understand why dad felt a certain longing for the way things had been back in the era of the railroad, and why he was so determined to salvage whatever small part of it he could, before it completely vanished.

Walking west through town was always a depressing experience. The buildings along Arlington became increasingly shabbier. Some of the shops had been boarded up, others turned into dwellings. The businesses that remained seemed almost out of place. Cut-rate clothing stores, junk shops, laundromats, and pool halls dominated. The color seemed to have drained out of everything. Even the faces of the people she passed were stark and drawn. Men sat in the entranceways to boarded buildings or congregated on the corners. She felt their eyes on her as she passed.

Once she took the turn onto Vintner she felt a little better. Here old trees arched over the narrow street, shading it completely. Most of the houses had been built before the turn of the century for the workers on the railroad. They were two-story row houses with flat roofs and postage-stamp lawns for the most part. The owners had painted the bricks bright colors and most of the places were well kept. An old woman, nearly bent double by arthritis, was out tending her rose bushes. The whole of her front yard was given over to them. As Emily passed, the woman turned from her work and her ancient face broke into a smile.

There were only about a dozen houses on the bend in the road opposite the depot. One of them had to be the house where Miss Potts lived. But which one? She walked slowly past them considering each one closely, eliminating some instantly.

A group of boys were playing baseball on the road. The seams on the ball were starting to come undone so that when someone hit it the ball flapped rather than rolled along the road. A boy with short-cropped blond hair was standing on the sidewalk in front of one of the houses. He edged his tee shirt, which doubled as third base, out of the way to let her pass.

"Excuse me," she said. He kept his eyes firmly riveted on the batter at the plate. "Would you happen to know someone by the name of Potts?"

The boy showed no sign of having heard her. He slapped his fist into the glove and shouted encouragement to the pitcher. She went on to describe Miss Potts: small, sixtyish, gray hair done up in a bun. Finally the boy took his eyes off the game and turned to her.

"You don't live around here."

"No."

"Yeah, you don't look like you live around here. Listen, this place is crawling with old ladies. There's more old ladies around here than kids. I can't tell one from the other. Now would you mind moving, you're standing on third base."

"Please, this is important. She must live in one of these houses right here."

"Way to go, Whitey," shouted the boy. The batter had just struck out. He slammed the bat down onto the road in disgust. The boy turned to her again. "Look, why don't you try that house over there. There's a whole bunch of them in there. Maybe one of them's the one you're looking for."

"Thanks. You've been a big help."

"Yeah, sure." He turned back to the game again. "Okay, Whitey. Just one more out, big guy."

The house the boy had pointed to was one of the few three-story houses on the block. It was a white frame building with green trim around the windows.

A porch ran across the front of the house, with an awning to keep off the sun. At one end of the porch there was a swing. Grass and hedge had both recently been cut. The whole place had a fussy look about it.

She moved slowly up the walk and onto the porch. The door knocker was in the shape of a lion's paw. It made a very serious sound as it struck the wood. No one answered.

She was about to knock again when the door edged open and a thin, bald head peeked out. A man peered down through thick glasses at her. He seemed disappointed to discover it was only a girl on the other side.

"Excuse me," she began. "I'm looking for a Miss Potts. Does she live here?"

He studied her silently for a second, cocking his head slightly to one side, as if she was speaking a foreign language. She started to repeat the question.

"Are you one of her students?" he asked. He was not exactly unfriendly, just painfully formal.

"Yes, that's right. May I speak to her, please?"

"Who shall I say is calling?"

"Emily Endicott." He closed the door quietly in her face. Behind her the baseball game continued. Whitey had just struck out another batter when the door opened again.

"Come in," said the tall man. "My name is Mr. Palmer. Miss Potts asked that I show you up to her room."

Emily followed him through the hall and up a wide, dark staircase. The wood of the staircase was slightly scooped in the center where countless feet had trod, the railing lighter where years of hands had held it. Glancing over the bannister on the way up she had seen into a large, dim room where two

100

rather odd-looking people stared up at her from the edge of an enormous sofa.

Mr. Palmer rapped lightly on the door at the head of the stairs, then opened it. He stood aside to let Emily enter. It was a small room, comfortably cluttered, after the fashion of an earlier age. The bed dominated, looking somehow out of place, as though it had wandered in from another room and forgotten the way out. Miss Potts was sitting on the far side of the room at a small drop-leaf desk.

"Emily," she said, as she glanced up and saw her there. "How good of you to drop by." Beneath the cheerful surface Emily sensed a tension in her words. "Come on in," she went on, rising from the desk to greet her. "Perhaps you could put the kettle on for tea, Mr. Palmer."

As soon as he had gone, Miss Potts' tone changed abruptly. The enforced cheerfulness disappeared from her voice. In its place there was obvious concern.

"Is everything all right, my dear?" she said, taking Emily's arm and leading her over to the window seat. "How on earth did you find me here?"

They sat down and Emily proceeded to tell her about father's visit to the depot last night and the mysterious woman in the doorway, whom he had seen disappear into one of the houses opposite.

Miss Potts nodded. "So that was your father," she said quietly.

"Yes," said Emily. "And you were the woman?"

Miss Potts looked at her and smiled weakly. It was obvious to Emily that she was worried to death. There were dark circles around her eyes. She seemed on edge, preoccupied. Her eyes darted suddenly to the door. A second later there was a slight rap at it.

"Come in," she called.

The door opened and a small birdlike woman with wooly white hair and quick furtive eyes came in carrying a tray. Emily recognized her as one of the women who had been sitting on the sofa downstairs.

"Here's your tea," she said. "Where shall I put it?"

"You can just leave it on the table by the bed, Mrs. Holmes. Thank you."

"Oh, no trouble at all, no trouble at all. There are some cookies as well. I just baked them this morning."

"Lovely."

"They're chocolate chip."

"Yes, thank you, Mrs. Holmes." But Mrs. Holmes showed no signs of leaving. She had stationed herself by the bed, hands folded in front of her, and was smiling sweetly at them.

"This is Emily Endicott," said Miss Potts finally. "A student of mine from the school." She had risen from the window seat and was advancing upon Mrs. Holmes.

"How nice," said Mrs. Holmes. "So good to see a young face around the house."

"We were just discussing a little project Emily has been working on over the summer." She had Mrs. Holmes by the elbow now and was guiding her gently but firmly toward the door.

"I see," said Mrs. Holmes. "Well, I suppose I should be running along now. If you need anything else—"

"We'll call you. Thank you, Mrs. Holmes." She closed the door quietly and put on the hook. Then she turned to Emily and put her finger to her lips.

There were a few seconds' silence. Finally, just outside the door there was a telltale squeak of floorboards followed by a sudden flurry of footsteps on the stairs.

"Mrs. Holmes abhors a mystery," explained Miss Potts, bringing the tray over to the window seat. She put the tray down between them and poured the steaming tea into fluted pink cups. Emily noticed her hand trembling slightly as she passed her one of them.

"Now," she said. "Where were we? Oh yes, I remember. We were talking about last night. Yes, that was me at the depot. I saw a light on in there and I thought—well, never mind what I thought. I'm really very glad to see you. I'd been thinking of phoning you tonight, actually. The mystery of the handbill has deepened considerably since we spoke last week. But tell me, what brings you here today? Was it simply to see whether the crazy woman your father saw last night was me?"

"No, that wasn't all. My father found something when he was there last night."

"Yes. What did he find?"

"Another of the handbills."

Miss Potts had been going through the cookies on the tray, turning them over one by one to inspect the undersides, all of which were burned. She looked up at Emily.

"You're sure?" she said.

"Yes. I saw it myself."

"You don't have it now?"

"No. He put it away. He was fascinated by it. I think he's planning on using it somehow in the exhibition. And there's something else."

She went on to explain her own experience at the

depot with Albert. Miss Potts sipped at her tea and stared silently out the window while she was talking.

"Well," she said, when Emily had finished, "I can't say that I'm really surprised. Everything you've told me simply confirms my fears. Come here. I'd like to show you something. I was just looking at this before you came."

She led Emily over to the drop-leaf desk. There was a large, old book opened on it, with a magnifying glass lying across the book.

"This is a volume of the old *Encyclopaedia Britannica* Miss Blight keeps in the living room." She sat down in the chair and picked up the maginifying glass. "And this here," she said, indicating the page the book was opened to, "is what is called a Perpetual Calendar. It will tell you on what day a given date fell in any year."

Emily looked over Miss Pott's shoulder at the book. At the top of the left-hand page there was column upon column of years, from the year 1791 to the year 2050. Beside each one there was a number, from 1 to 14. The numbers referred to a series of numbered calendars printed on the two pages.

"Last night," said Miss Potts, "I noticed something unusual. I realized that the eighth of August this year fell on a Saturday. That is the date of the show on the handbill, and back then it fell on a Saturday as well. After I got back from my little episode at the depot I decided to look this up. My feeling was that since coincidence of day and date must occur fairly frequently it probably didn't mean much. That was what I wanted to believe, at any rate. But look here."

She trained the magnifying glass over the column of dates. "As you can see, for 1936, the year of the show, we are referred to calendar number 11, one of the special leap year calendars. We are directed to the same calendar again for this year. And the only other year between then and now that is also keyed to calendar number 11, is the year 1964." She put aside the magnifying glass and turned to Emily. "Now, doesn't it strike you as a rather remarkable coincidence that this old playbill should suddenly turn up again in the very year that finds day and date aligning as they did then?"

She closed the book, stood up, and slowly walked to the window, where she looked out silently across the field. Two men from the society were busy ripping up the rotted planks from the platform and replacing them with new ones. The hammer would strike, and a couple of seconds later the sound would bounce off the back of the house.

"Suppose there is a door," said Miss Potts, half to herself, "a door separating this day-to-day world of ours from another, darker realm. Say that for the most part that door is closed—perhaps we do not even know it is there—but now and then, at certain times, in certain places, it suddenly swings open. Perhaps they would be places where darkness once passed, setting its stamp indelibly upon that spot, casting its long shadow down through time."

The hammer's echo throbbed eerily against the house. Miss Potts turned from the window to face Emily. "Perhaps this depot is such a place," she said. "And perhaps that show was such a darkness."

Emily stood dumbfounded, gripping the back of the chair. She wanted to shout out, laugh, anything to shatter the horrible feeling of foreboding that had settled over the room.

"What are you saying?" she said. "That

something is about to happen at the depot? But what? How?''

''I don't know, my dear. All I have is this feeling, this dreadful feeling that a door is about to burst open. Tomorrow I will go down to the library to look through the back files of the *Caledon Daily* for August 1964. That will be the test. I was not in Caledon then myself. I had taken a position at a girl's boarding school back East and was out of touch with news here for a number of years. But it seems to me that the fire that finally closed the station for good occurred in that year.''

''Yes, that's right. Father's spoken about it several times.''

''I am looking for something that happened in August of that year. If there is nothing there, then I will be ready and more than willing to abandon all this foolishness of mine. I will take the handbill, tear it into tiny pieces, and flush it down the toilet. Then I will pack my suitcase, head for the nearest airport, and catch the next flight south to some island beach where there is nothing to do but lie in the sun all day and scorch.''

''Would it be all right if I came with you tomorrow?''

''You're sure you want to, Emily?''

''Yes, I'm sure.''

''In that case, I'm sure another set of eyes would be a great help. Mine aren't getting any better with age, and the print in those papers is impossible. Well now, that's enough of all this nonsense for a while. There's still some more tea in the pot, if it's not stone cold by now. And I've got a lovely tin of biscuits in the closet.''

They were soon sitting on the edge of the bed, sipping tea and finishing up the last of the foil-

106

wrapped cookies in the tin. They talked about family and school and friends, anything other than the task at hand. And for a time they were almost able to forget the depot, and the handbill, and the Children's Show.

Yet still the dull, persistent thud of the hammer continued in the distance. And more than once Miss Potts glanced up at the calendar and silently counted down the six short days until the eighth of August.

Chapter 17

It was wet and windy the following day, and the library was full to overflowing with kids looking for something to do. Miss Oberon, the librarian, was going out of her mind. She had finally barricaded herself in her office, where she buried her head in the pages of *Library Journal* and pretended all this wasn't really happening.

Emily and Miss Potts had left their umbrellas just inside the door to drip. There were about two dozen others along with them, but Emily would have no problem recognizing hers when it was time to leave. It was a massive green-and-gold golf umbrella that mother had bought for a steal at one of the bargain houses she haunted. The thing weighed about fifty pounds and needed two hands just to keep it aloft. If a good wind ever got it you'd either break both arms or lift off.

Now, as Miss Potts flipped through the card catalog, Emily was still trying to rub the feeling back into her wrists.

"Here we are," said Miss Potts. "The *Caledon Daily Examiner*. It says they have a complete run of the paper back as far as 1929, and broken volumes before that. The card is stamped 'Desk.' We'll have to ask the librarian to get it for us."

It took half a dozen rings of the hand bell on the

check-out desk before Miss Oberon looked up from her magazine. When she saw Miss Potts standing there her expression brightened, and she made her way quickly to the counter. Finally someone was going to ask her for something other than the key to the bathroom.

"Yes," she said. "Can I help you?" She already had her pencil between her teeth and her eyes narrowed, ready to field a tough reference question.

Miss Potts said she was looking for the 1964 volume of the *Caledon Daily*. The pencil dropped to the floor and the eyes closed. She took a deep sigh and glanced over toward the front door where a bunch of rowdies were taking face pictures on the photocopy machine.

"You'll have to wait for a few minutes," she said. "They're down in the basement stacks."

"Fine," said Miss Potts. "We'll just wait at that table over there."

Ten minutes later Miss Oberon reappeared, panting. She was carrying a huge, dusty tome, which she thumped down on the table in front of them.

"Thank you," said Miss Potts sweetly, as the librarian walked grimly away, brushing the dust from the front of her dress. A sharp, musty odor greeted them as they opened the volume.

"I'll bet no one's looked at these since they had them bound," said Miss Potts. She began leafing through the brittle, yellowed pages. Being in a damp basement for nearly thirty years certainly hadn't helped the cheap newsprint. The edges of the pages flaked off if you looked at them the wrong way.

As they fanned carefully through the volume, headlines flashed out at them, "Clay Defeats Liston," "Ruby Convicted in Oswald Murder,"

"Three Civil Rights Workers Slain in Mississippi," "Civil Rights Bill Becomes Law."

In August a new word began to dominate the front pages. Vietnam. "U.S. Aircraft Bomb North Vietnamese Bases," "Congress Supports President's Step," "South Vietnam Placed in State of Emergency."

By this point Miss Potts was muttering beneath her breath. She flipped quickly through pages, pausing only briefly when they reached the issue for Saturday, August 8.

"There won't be anything here," she said. "It's Monday's paper we should look at. Had anything unusual happened at the depot that Saturday, it would have been reported then." Nonetheless, they went page by page through Saturday's paper. They found this item in with the local news.

COMMUTER SERVICE SUSPENDED

As a result of the recent fire that caused extensive damage to the Caledon Depot and forced the closing of the building, daily rail commuter service has been temporarily suspended.

For past few years the operation has been running at a deficit, and a spokesman for the Interurban Transit Authority suggests that the future of the service is now under review.

The cause of the fire is still under investigation.

The headline for the tenth read "Turkey Invades Cyprus." They began to leaf slowly through the paper, Miss Potts hovering over the page, squinting as she ran her finger down the columns. "Daughter Saves

110

Invalid Mother From Flames," "Cruise Car Nabs Stolen Auto," "Crops Poor in Erin County," "Championship Won by Caledon Fiddler," "Phillies Down Mets," "Miss Beeton to Wed Today."

"I don't understand," said Miss Potts. "There must be something here. There has to be." She flipped quickly through the remainder of the paper: business news, stock exchange reports, classifieds, seeking out the small incidental items tucked among the back pages.

"Nothing," she said finally, taking off her glasses and rubbing her eyes. "Not one word." She slumped back in her chair. "Perhaps you could take another look, Emily, just in case I missed something. My eyes are killing me. I'll just sit here and rest them for a while."

Emily made her way slowly through the paper again, but there was simply no mention of the depot or anything else that might possibly support Miss Potts's suspicions. At one point she turned a page and swore for an instant that the word *Depot* flashed up at her. She went through the page three times, searching for it without success, and finally deciding that she must have imagined it.

Miss Potts was sitting beside her with her eyes closed and her chin resting in her hands. Her glasses lay on the table in front of her. She was the perfect picture of dejection. Looking at her now, Emily felt it was no wonder the others in the house were concerned about her. The transformation she had undergone in the month and a half since school ended was truly remarkable.

Emily felt conflicting emotions at having found nothing. On the one hand she was glad, relieved to know that the theory was not in fact true, with all the horrific consequences that would have entailed.

111

But on the other, she felt sad for Miss Potts's sake and desperately concerned about her. She seemed like someone poised on the edge of a nervous breakdown. It would certainly have been better for her if they *had* found something.

As she glanced up from the paper to break the bad news, her eye wandered across the ranges of bookstacks on the far side of the room and fell upon a somehow familiar figure. For some reason the sight of him there tensed her stomach and sent a whisper of fear up her spine. She found herself getting out of the chair.

"I'll be right back, Miss Potts," she said. "I think there's someone I know over there." As she crossed the carpeted room her legs felt weak and rubbery as though they might buckle beneath her.

As she came closer, the figure, which until now had been squatting in front of one of the lower shelves, stood suddenly. It was a strange, almost mechanical motion, as was the quick swing of the head as it turned to face her.

She stopped in her tracks as the pale, chiseled face of Scott Renshaw fixed her in its gaze. The crack of a smile appeared.

She felt unable to move, unable even to think. She may have stood there for a few seconds, or a few minutes. She couldn't say. Time washed over and around her, but did not touch her. Finally, he turned away.

And in that instant she suddenly remembered something, something she had completely forgotten about until just then. It had happened on the final day of classes. She had been out in the yard at recess, reading, and for some reason her eye had been drawn to the windows of their classroom on the third floor. The blinds were half drawn to keep out the sun, and the sills were lined with Miss Potts's plants. Standing at one of the windows, was Scott Renshaw, the new boy. He was looking off into the distance at something.

She couldn't figure out what he was doing up there at all. Perhaps Miss Potts had kept him in for some reason. She stood looking up at him for a few minutes, wondering what it could be he was studying so intently. Suddenly, as if aware of her scrutiny, he had swung his head down and stared directly at her, and that same chilling smile had flickered on his face.

He walked slowly down the aisle now, and disappeared around the end of the stacks.

Emily hurried across the room after him. She looked down first one row, then another, but he was nowhere to be seen. It was as though he had vanished into thin air. As she walked slowly back to Miss Potts, Emily paused before the shelf where she had first seen him. There were half a dozen books on the bottom shelf. All of them were books on magic.

Miss Potts had managed to pull herself together somewhat by the time Emily got back. She wore an enforced cheerful smile and sat with her hands folded on the closed volume of newspapers.

"Find who you were looking for?" she asked.

"No," said Emily, glancing back over her shoulder. "I thought I saw someone, but I must have been mistaken."

"I know the feeling. Well, there's no point hanging about here any longer, I suppose. Give me a hand with this monster, will you?"

They lugged the book back to the counter and set it down with a thud. There was no sign of Miss Oberon at all now. She had probably seen them coming and ducked under the desk.

It had stopped raining, at least. While Emily folded the still-damp umbrella and struggled with the snap, Miss Potts plodded along beside her, plowing through the puddles with abandon.

"What an old fool I am," she said finally. "I should be delighted that we found nothing in that paper. In fact, I should be ecstatic. But that's not at all the way I feel. I feel depressed and disappointed. Here I thought I'd latched onto the key to the puzzle, and I was completely wrong. I was so sure that we were going to find something in those papers that I'd have staked my life on it. Oh well, if all of this has done anything at all, it's probably convinced you once and for all that I'm completely out of my mind."

She turned to Emily, who was walking with her head down and her hands folded behind her back, dragging the umbrella along in tow. "Why so glum?" she asked. "Don't tell me you're disappointed too?"

"No," said Emily, "it's not that. It's just that when we were back there in the library I did see someone. I saw Scott Renshaw, but when I went to look for him I couldn't find him."

"Oh," said Miss Potts suddenly, remembering the strange sensation she had had the other day, the feeling that he was sitting in the classroom with her.

"And I remembered something that had happened on the last day of classes," continued Emily, and she went on to tell Miss Potts how she had seen him standing in the window, staring off into the distance. "I thought you might have kept him in for some reason, and I guess I just forgot about the whole thing until now."

"No," said Miss Potts. "I hadn't kept him in. As I recall, there was a party in the teachers' lounge that morning. The class was empty when I left it."

114

"You know," said Emily, "it probably doesn't mean anything, but it was right after we got in from recess that I found the handbill on my desk."

Later that day, after she and Emily had parted, promising to be in touch sometime during the coming week, Miss Potts dropped in at the school. She went up to her room and looked through her book. She found Scott Renshaw's name, and jotted down the phone number and address she had penciled in hurriedly beside his name on that day he first came to her class. Then she stood for a long while at the window, clutching the piece of paper in her hand and staring off into the distance as Scott Renshaw had done that day.

She knew the view perfectly well, of course, without having to stand there, but she did so all the same. In the winter when the trees shed their leaves she was able to see all the way to Arlington Avenue on a clear day. Now, though, a green cloud of foliage had settled over the town. Only a few prominent landmarks stood out: Saint Stephen's Church, with its steeple rising high above the trees; Holy Cross Cemetery on the rise of land at the eastern edge of town; a couple of new apartment buildings; and an office tower downtown, its glass and steel flanks gleaming in the late afternoon sun. It may have been any one of these that had attracted Scott Renshaw's gaze that day. It may have been, but she did not think it was any of them.

Her eye followed the bend of the Bedford Ravine, a dark green snake twisting through the town. From here she could clearly see the ancient trestle that spanned the ravine at the western end. And just beside it, its newly polished copper roof ablaze with sunlight, the depot.

Chapter 18

A faint breeze played about the lace curtains. In the yard below, Miss Potts could hear the ridiculous bark of Samantha next door as the back gate shut and something slithered over the patio stone. She glanced down and discovered Mr. Palmer walking the sprinkler to the far end of the yard to begin the evening watering.

You could punch a clock by the progress of Mr. Palmer's sprinkler around the grounds during the course of the day. Being a military man, Mr. Palmer was a creature of habit. Mornings, directly after breakfast, he would begin on the front yard, finishing by noon. He would not water in the afternoon, as the sun was too hot then and the grass would scorch. Instead he would tend to his gardening, going busily through the beds like a doctor making his rounds. In the evening, after dinner, he would set the sprinkler out in the backyard, gradually working it up toward the house. Now he walked back past the still-barking dog to turn the hose on. The delicate plume of water fanned back and forth over the clipped green grass, the fine mist shot with the dull gold of the late sun. Miss Potts's eye wandered past the arc, past the rippling field of grass beyond, until it rested on the station.

The transformation was now almost complete.

Today again, shortly after seven o'clock, she had been awakened by the work crew banging around the place. They had been working on the windows for the past few days, removing the boards and shutters from the ground floor frames, smashing what remained of the old glass and replacing it with new. The upper windows would come later, as would work on the upper floor in general. The fire there some years back had fairly gutted the floor and major structural rebuilding was necessary. For now the funds at hand were going exclusively to the refurbishing of the main floor of the building.

Today they had put in place two new curved panes of glass in the waiting room windows. The effect was uncanny. While before the shuttered windows had seemed at times like eyes lowered in sleep, now they looked like nothing so much as those same eyes suddenly opened. It was as though the depot had been stirred in its slumber, had roused and shaken off the dust and dirt of age, and stood again as it had when Miss Potts was a girl.

She had attempted several times during the day to get in touch with Scott Renshaw. Only ten minutes earlier she had again dialed the number copied from her book. With again the same result—no answer. Only the hollow trill of the phone across the wires.

She pretended to be annoyed, but in fact she was more than a little glad. For she did not particularly relish the prospect of confronting Scott Renshaw about the handbill. There was something definitely wrong with the boy, an undercurrent of violence that belied his frail appearance. It was stamped in the cold dispassion of those eyes, carved in the mocking twist of that mouth. She remembered again the chill that had run through her the other day in the empty classroom as she stared down at the empty desk.

117

One part of her wanted desperately to believe that this boy, a stranger to Caledon, could not possibly know anything about the handbill, and his presence in the room that recess had a purely reasonable explanation. But another part of her had long since cast logic and reasonableness aside. That part plumbed that icy stare and saw something unthinkable there. That part pictured him standing impassively at the window staring over at the depot, and felt a chill at the bone.

Fifteen minutes later Mr. Palmer reappeared, walked the length of the yard, and moved the sprinkler ten paces closer to the house. Miss Potts watched him from the window as she held the phone to her ear and listened to the relentless and somehow sinister ringing on the other end.

Mother had mounted the calendar over the stove. A grease pencil tied to a piece of string hung from the same nail that supported the calendar. Every evening after Albert and Elizabeth and Charles had been bathed and put to bed mother went to the kitchen, took the cotton balls from her ears, and dropped them into the egg cup on the back of the stove, then reached up and crossed off the day on the calendar with the grease pencil. As the summer wore on, the crosses got darker. It reminded Emily of a prisoner counting down the days of his sentence. For some reason, though, she had forgotten to cross off yesterday's date.

Emily reached up, deliberately ran the pencil twice in an x through the 4, then took the pot of tea she had prepared and headed downstairs. The rest of the family were out. Father, in a rare moment of lucidity, had suddenly realized that between his work on the layout and the final stages of the renovations

118

on the depot, time with the family had dwindled to nil. Mother's sanity, tenuous at the best of times, was dangling by a frayed thread at this point. Last night over dinner she had threatened to plant a bomb at the depot. Later in the evening Mr. Endicott had made a phone call to change his plans for today, and first thing this morning they had packed up the car and headed off for a day at the beach. Emily, seizing upon the opportunity for a little solitude, had chanced upon a touch of flu and remained at home.

Poor Miss Potts, Emily thought. In the light of day all her talk about the magic show and the mysterious handbill paled a little. The trip to the library had really settled it for Emily. She was more than ready for a good strong dose of the "real world." Still, things would be much better for everyone once this week was over.

There was a crisp rap at the side door. She went to get it. One peek through the curtains at the bleached blond head on the other side and she knew who it was.

"Hello, Lydia," she said as she opened the door. Lydia was standing there in her metalic blue bikini, admiring her tan. She had a bowl in one hand and a cigarette in the other.

"Oh, hi, Emmy. How are you? Mind if I step in?"

Lydia lived in the bungalow next door. They shared the narrow alley between the houses, and their kitchen windows looked directly into one another. This was quite a treat, since Lydia wasn't too particular about what she wore around the house. Lydia really didn't need any admirers, though. She already knew she was about the most beautiful specimen to hit the planet in quite some time.

"Ooo," she cooed, "it's nice and cool in here. My place is like an oven."

"Have you ever considered curtains?"

"Pardon?"

"Nothing. Been sunbathing?" It was a ridiculous question. Lydia practically lived on the chaise longue in her backyard from May to September.

"Yeah," she pouted, looking at her chest, "but I think it's going to peel." She was looking around the room for somewhere to flick her ash. She settled for the floor. "Em, could you be a doll and lend me some ice. My freezer's on the fritz and I'm just dying for a drink."

"Sure, hang on and I'll see if we've got some." The frost-encrusted ice cube tray was buried under about ten pounds of lean ground, last week's special at the supermarket. She finally managed to extract it and ran it under hot water to loosen the cubes.

"Oh, that's just super, Em. Here, I brought a bowl." This time she flicked the ash in the sink. "I swear I don't know how you all manage to fit in here. I'd go right out of my mind."

There was no point in pursuing *that*. Emily handed her the bowl of ice. "We sleep standing up," she said.

"Umm?"

"Forget it."

As Lydia moved her tan out into the alley she turned. "Thanks a bunch, Emmy. If you ever need anything you know where to knock." She moved off down the alley with the slow studied walk of a model on a runway and disappeared into her backyard.

Welcome to the real world.

* * *

He didn't dare go up the fire escape anymore, for fear the tattooed man would find him there. Instead, he parked his bike out of sight and dropped down into one of the yards on the other side of the lane within view of the apartment. There he crouched in a narrow space between a row of rose bushes that ran across the back of the yard and the low retaining wall that kept the lane at bay. The top of the wall was level with the lane, and periodically he would peer cautiously over the edge of it at the apartment window, looking for signs of life. There were none.

He stayed there for hours that day and again the next, until the backs of his legs ached from squatting in the cramped space and his arms were covered in scratches from the rose bushes.

By Thursday he was growing desperate. The idea had rooted itself in his mind that Scott was somehow punishing him for the theft of the book. All he wanted was the chance to see him again, to explain that it had all been a big mistake, to accept the consequences whatever they might be. Anything to end this awful void he felt inside, and to get things back to the way they had been before.

But there was no sign of Scott. It was as if he'd dropped right off the face of the earth.

Chapter 19

The Children's Show

III

"And now," said the magician, *"may I have a volunteer from the audience?"* Arms went up around the room. *"Remember, each and every one of you who assists the professor will receive a copy of this illuminating little volume I hold here in my hand. Learn how you too can unlock the mysteries of time and space. Amaze your friends and family.*

"Yes, the little girl in the back there. Come along, sweetheart, don't be bashful. There's nothing to be afraid of. The professor won't bite."

A skinny little girl in a pale yellow pinafore slowly made her way up the aisle. Her face was dirty and she wore no shoes. She had probably come from the squatters' camp outside of town. There was a look of hunger and fear in her eyes.

As she climbed the makeshift stairs, the magician extended his hand to her. "Let's give the little lady a nice hand," he said and showed her over to a low stool in the center of the stage. He helped her up onto the stool, then extended her arms from her sides, placing an upright pole under each of them close to her body.

"Now," said the magician, as he uncorked a bottle filled with a yellowish solution and held it under the girl's nose, "when this liquid is at its highest concentration, if a living being breathes it, the body becomes in a matter of moments as light as air."

The unmistakable odor of ether drifted through the room. The girl's eyes gradually closed, and her head dropped forward. Her knees began to sag. The magician bent down and took away the stool. The girl hung in the air, supported only by the poles under her arms.

Working very carefully, the magician bent the girl's right arm until the hand touched the head. Then he gently removed the rod from under her left arm. The remaining rod did not topple. The girl slept quietly on, resting on the single pole.

Finally, with a single finger, the magician lifted the girl's feet until the body was horizontal in the air. With a slight kick of his foot he dislodged the one remaining pole. It clattered to the floor of the stage. A gasp ran through the room.

The girl slept on in the empty air.

Chapter 20

Thursday had come and gone, and Miss Potts had still not managed to get in touch with Scott Renshaw. It was long past midnight now and she was sitting in her room listening to the mellow rumble of the radio and keeping one eye on the depot. A tight knot of anxiety had planted itself in the pit of her stomach, which no amount of self-reproof would loosen. What did she hope to gain by exhausting herself with this absurd vigil? She would wind up in the hospital if she kept it up. The others in the house, obviously worried about her, were already pressing to have a doctor look at her. Why could she not simply leave go of this ridiculous fantasy she had concocted? But, no, as the clock ticked inexorably toward the eighth of August, she grew increasingly anxious, convinced that some dark, malefic force was poised to pounce upon them.

Once again her thoughts were full of the Children's Show, as were her dreams. That, more than anything else, was what kept her from her bed these nights. She no sooner closed her eyes than the professor, with his smooth, terrifying voice, would begin whispering in her ear. She would awake in the morning feeling empty and drained, as if he had silently sucked the life from her while she slept.

Perhaps a drink would help to calm her nerves,

she thought, laying aside the book she had plucked randomly from the shelf earlier in the evening. The brandy bottle was on top of the bureau where it had sat quietly gathering dust since the last of her infrequent tipples. Her birthday, that had been, when a glass or two had helped her realize how glad she should be to be growing old. She crossed the creaky floor and reached over her head, feeling blindly around for the squat brown bottle.

Before she managed to find it, however, her hand fell upon the photo albums. It lingered there, seemingly of its own accord, refusing to move until she finally took hold of the top one and lifted it down. With it and the brandy bottle she went back to the window seat.

She emptied what remained of her tea into the hibiscus plant on the sill, then filled the cup half full of brandy and took a sip. Several sips later the knot in her stomach felt considerably looser than it had in some time and she took up the photo album, determined to take the handbill from it and tear it into the tiny pieces she had promised she would.

She flipped through the album and found it, neatly folded and tucked among the early photographs in the book. Yet no sooner had the night air touched it than an incredible thing occurred. The handbill began to disintegrate.

Like the perfect ash of a cigarette that has been allowed to burn down undisturbed, it appeared substantial, but as soon as she touched it it fell to dust, scattering down onto the window seat and the floor.

She stared down in disbelief. Directly beneath the place where the handbill had lain there was a photo, an old sepia-tinted photo her father had taken when she was a girl. It was labeled, "A Trip to the Country—August, 1936." She remembered the occasion quite clearly. They had all gone for an outing on the excursion train that ran weekly through town in the summer, taking picnic-laden families to the countryside for the day.

The photo showed her mother and herself standing on the platform of the station, waiting for the train. Mother was wearing a long belted linen suit and a small flowered straw hat. The camera had caught her with one hand shielding her eyes, looking down the line for the train. She, herself, was sitting on the big wicker basket at her mother's feet, staring shyly into the camera, she wore a polka dot Shirley Temple dress, and her hair too, all in curls, was patterned after the child star.

In the background there were a number of other families also standing waiting for the train. But it was not these that now caught her attention as she looked at the photo. Instead it was a solitary figure that her eyes fastened upon: a boy, leaning against the wall of the depot. He wore a loose white shirt folded up to the elbows and short pants with suspenders. He was carrying what appeared to be a sheaf of handbills under his arm and he seemed to be staring directly into the camera.

There was something about the pose the boy struck, leaning there with one leg up against the building, that seemed disturbingly familiar to Miss Potts. But the boy was in the background of the picture, and she was unable to make out the details of his face.

She went to get the magnifying glass from her desk. Training the lens on the figure in the photograph, she looked down into the glass and brought it slowly into focus. At first a whitish blur, the features took sudden shape. There, staring out at her

126

across a half a century, she saw the lean, smiling face of Scott Renshaw.

Miss Potts pushed open the beauty salon door and went in. A buzzer immediately began to sound, continuing until the door had closed itself behind her. The shop was empty. A drift of blond hair lay on the floor around one of the chairs. A bank of bubbletop dryers ran along one wall, with stacks of dogeared magazines piled on low tables between them. A curtain parted at the back of the shop, and a woman poked her head out.

"Oh, hi," she said around a wad of gum. "Thought I heard the bell. Be with you in a jiff."

It was Friday afternoon. All morning Miss Potts had been glued to the phone, dialing the same futile number over and over again. Finally she had given up and decided to look up the address the boy had given as his home. She had toyed briefly with the idea of phoning Emily, but the strong feeling of foreboding she had about the visit had stopped her.

Again the curtain opened and the woman emerged. She was short and slight and wore a powder blue uniform that needed a wash.

"Sorry to keep you waiting," she said. "I was on the phone. Do you have an appointment?"

"No," said Miss Potts. "Actually, I'm not sure I have the correct address. I was looking for the Renshaws. This is 903 Arlington, isn't it?"

"Yes, that's right, but there's no one by that name here. Maybe you want the apartments up top. We get their mail lots of times. I don't remember that name, though. Renshaw, you say, eh? Funny, rings a bell." She got a broom from behind the counter and began sweeping up the hair around the chair. "How about

127

a quick wash and set while you're here? Special for seniors this week. Maybe a nice rinse?''

"No, thank you," said Miss Potts. "But perhaps you could show me how I find these apartments.''

"Sure.'' She pointed out the front window of the shop. "It's that door right out there, to the left. That's right.''

"Thank you," said Miss Potts over the sound of the buzzer as she opened the door.

"No trouble at all. Renshaw? It'll come to me, I know.''

The entranceway was close and cramped. Handbills and cigarette butts littered the floor. The stairway directly in front of her launched off into the dimness of the upper floor. Taking a deep, labored breath, Miss Potts started up the stairs.

She rested awhile on the top stair, her hand clutching the wobbly handrail, and wondered for more than the first time if she'd done the right thing in coming here.

Ahead of her lay a narrow, high-ceiled hallway with a bare, low-wattage bulb illumining it. The tile floor was dull with dirt. Her eye fell on a door at the end of the hall facing her. The air in her lungs froze momentarily, and she realized that here lay the end of her search for Scott Renshaw.

"Come on, old girl," she scolded herself. "You've come this far. There's no turning back now.'' Her feet would not listen. They remained firmly rooted to the top stair. Finally it was sheer force of will that drew them reluctantly down the hall.

She rapped sharply on the door, coughing and straightening her skirt. "Hello," she rehearsed to herself, "my name is Irma Potts. I'm your son's teacher at the school. I was wondering if Scott might

128

be in. No, no, it's nothing serious. I just had something to ask him. . . ."

There was no answer. She knocked again, this time noting a strange hollow sound to the knock. By now it was clear that there was no one home. She turned to leave.

She had taken but a few steps, however, when there was a quiet *click* behind her, and she turned to discover that the door had opened a crack. She went back.

"Hello," she called through the opening. "Is there anyone home?" Silence was the only reply. With a slight, reluctant pressure of her palm she pushed the door open.

She found herself looking down a long, empty hall that ran from one end of the apartment to the other. Several doors opened off the hall, the first but a few feet away. Fighting back an irresistible urge to turn and run, she edged her way tentatively down the hall until she came even with the first door. She looked in.

Suddenly she found herself in a park. One fork of the path she was on branched sharply off to the left. There was an arbor, thickly blanketed with rose bushes in bloom. The air was heavy with their perfume.

For an instant she felt confused, as though she had suddenly lost her way. There was something she had been thinking about a moment ago, something she had been about to do. For some reason she couldn't quite remember what it had been. Oh well, she thought, it mustn't have been that important. It would come to her later, no doubt. There was no point in letting it ruin her walk.

The weather was beautiful. Somewhere someone was burning something. The air had the acrid edge of smoke to it. She was strolling down a narrow, winding avenue lined with trees. The trees were unlike any she had ever seen, ancient and massive, the bark like hide hanging in slack folds from the trunks. The boughs met and meshed overhead like interlocking hands.

Glancing up, she realized that she could not see the sky for the thick canopy of leaves. As the breeze blew through the branches, the leaves made a loud, leathery rustle. Those that had fallen to the path crackled like brittle shells beneath her shoes. A faint ripple of unease ran through her. Instinctively she glanced behind.

Not ten feet away there was a low stone wall with a door in it. The wall was of fieldstone, mortared between. Spikes of broken glass mixed with mortar ran along the top of it.

It was a heavy wooden door, rounded at the top, with a large iron ring for a handle. The strange thing was that she couldn't remember having come through the door, though she must have done so just minutes before, since the path she was on ended abruptly before it. Looking back at it now, she suddenly had the queer conviction that if she were to go back there and open the door she would discover something very surprising on the other side. She had almost talked herself into doing just that when her attention was diverted from the door by a sound that came from further along the path. It was hard to place exactly what it was, but it struck some faint forgotten chord inside her.

Turning from the door, she started slowly along the path in the direction of the sound. A short distance ahead there was a slight bend in the path. As she approached the bend the sound grew gradually more distinct. It seemed to her now almost like the sound

130

of clapping, and she stopped suddenly, the thought again threatening to jar loose some distant memory.

Again the scent of roses was in the air. A large bush grew at the bend in the path, covered with blooms. They were the giant red hybrids her father used to grow in the garden when she was a girl. She hadn't seen one in years, and on impulse she broke a flower from the thick, spiked stem as she turned the corner.

She found herself in a circular clearing. There were benches ranged around the edge, while in the center there stood a large floral sundial. The shadow, she noticed, fell upon the eight.

On the far side of the clearing a gentleman whose back was to her was feeding bread crumbs to the pigeons from a large paper bag. Other than the two of them the area was deserted, and she could not figure out where the clapping she had heard could have come from.

She sat down on a bench nearby to rest, sniffing the intoxicating scent of the rose while she admired the considerable skill that had gone into creating the elaborate floral display.

Suddenly she heard the sound again, and looking over at the man, was surprised to see that what she had first taken to be pigeons were in fact large black birds, ravens of some sort, she supposed. They were perched on his shoulders, even his head, and the ground around his feet was thick with them. As he scattered the crumbs from the bag they would rise up in a sudden, startled flurry before settling back to feed. It was the dreadful snap of their huge wings that she had mistaken for clapping.

She tried to turn her attention back to the sundial, but now the stark scalloped shadow looked like nothing so much as an immense black wing falling over the flowers.

When she glanced over again there were twice as many birds as before. Where could they all have come from? And why did that horrid man keep feeding them? If it weren't absolutely insane, she would almost swear that they had sprung from the very crumbs he was strewing on the ground.

She was growing very nervous now. One of the birds had broken away from the rest and flown over to investigate her. It perched menacingly on the far end of the bench, fixing her with a hideous red eye.

She must get away from here—now. She edged over toward the end of the bench, slowly so as not to alarm the bird, and stood up. Immediately the awful creature let out a harsh, unearthly shriek, hardly a bird sound at all. She stiffened, and the hand that held the rose clenched into a sudden fist, the thorns biting deeply into her palm. She cried out in pain as the flower fell lazily to the ground.

Across the clearing the birds began to clamor. The figure in their midst stood fixed for an instant in the act of showering crumbs among them, and then with a smooth, almost mechanical motion he slowly turned to face her. She took one look at the gleeful white face and screamed. Her last memory before she fainted dead away was of a dark rush of wings swooping down on her.

She came to suddenly, blindly waving her arms about, battling shadows.

"Hey, take it easy, lady. Just take it easy. Everything's all right." She opened her eyes and found a massive man with small, frightened eyes bending over her. She was lying on the floor outside the door of the apartment, her head propped up on her purse.

132

"You all right, lady? Maybe I should call a doctor or something." The sweet smell of beer was on his breath. A grizzled stubble covered his cheeks and chin. Tattoos adorned his arms. She studied them in a detached sort of way as she waited for consciousness to fully return. Her eyes fell with curious alarm on one of an eagle with outstretched wings.

"Look, lady," said the man as he helped her to her feet. "I'm the superintendent of this place. What happened here anyway? One minute I'm sitting watching the tube, and the next thing I know there's this scream, and I run out and find you lying here."

Her head felt full of cobwebs. She struggled to think. "My name is Irma Potts," she said. "I'm a teacher. I was trying to find one of my students. He gave this as his address. I—I must have fallen or something." Her hand ached. She looked down at her palm and found it punctured as if by small, sharp teeth. Blood trickled from the wounds.

Suddenly she remembered the rose. And with it the rest flooded back in a dizzying rush. A dreadful whir of wings filled the air and for an instant she was staring again into the terrifying face of Professor Mephisto. She felt faint, and reached out blindly for the wall.

"Look, lady," said the fat man, taking her arm. "You better come with me, and we'll take care of that hand."

The inside of the apartment was dim and cluttered. A television with a set of twisted rabbit ears on top muttered to itself in the corner. In the open window a fan buzzed, while a thin, flowered curtain fluttered playfully near the blades. The man had cleared off a chair for her, throwing the pile of newspapers stacked on it onto a nearby couch, then fetching her a box of bandages and an ancient tube

133

of ointment. Now, as she tended to her wounds, she could hear him moving about in the kitchen, preparing her a cup of tea.

"The name's Henderson," he called through the door. "Like I said, I'm the super here. I'm supposed to clean up, keep an eye on the place for the owner, see? What do you want in the tea?"

"Nothing. Thank you." She watched the ghosts flit across the screen as she pressed a final bandage into place.

Mr. Henderson came back into the room, balancing two saucerless cups on a breadboard. Between the cups on the board there were two pieces of buttered white bread.

"How's the hand?" he said as he set the board down on a low table between them.

"Fine, thank you. Nothing serious."

"Here, help yourself." He picked up one of the cups and a piece of the bread and settled back onto the couch. "So you say you're a teacher, eh?"

"Yes, that's right. As I said, the student I was looking for gave this as his address. His name is Scott Renshaw." She leaned forward and picked up her cup, leaving the bread where it was.

"Renshaw, eh?" Mr. Henderson folded his bread in two and popped it into his mouth whole. He chewed thoughtfully for a few moments. "Well, do you want to know what I think, Miss—what did you say your name was?"

"Potts," she said, sipping tentatively at her tea. Mr. Henderson leaned forward and scooped up the second slice of bread.

"Right," he said. "Well, I think someone's been having a little game with you, Miss Potts. You see, that apartment there's empty. No one's lived there for a long, long time."

134

Chapter 21

"Emily. Time to get up, dear. It's nearly nine thirty. I have to go downtown, remember?"

Emily groaned and turned in the bed, mother's voice instantly fading into the dream. She was in the schoolyard again, staring up at Miss Potts's window. Scott Renshaw was standing there, but there was something different about him now. He seemed taller, older, his face so pale as to appear almost luminous. And when he turned to look at her she felt as if—

"Emily. Are you up yet? I want to wash my hair before I go."

"Yes," she said, through a mouth that felt as though it belonged to someone else. She pushed herself up in the bed and swung her legs over the side. Her head bobbed on her neck like Albert's jack-in-the-box.

She kicked into her slippers and went to wash her face at the laundry tubs, drying herself with the towel she kept slung over a pipe. Working the sleep from the corners of her eyes, she headed upstairs.

The kitchen, as usual, was pure pandemonium. Against the backdrop of the omnipresent television, the rumbling of the radio on the kitchen counter, and the frantic whistling of the kettle, another domestic catastrophe was unfolding.

Mother was safely closeted in the bathroom, her head stuck under the bathtub tap, washing her hair. You could hear her singing show tunes over the din of running water. Before she went in she had calmly sat the young ones down to cereal and juice. One bowl for Elizabeth, one for Charles, and three lined up on the table in front of Albert. In reality there was no more in Albert's three bowls combined than there was in either of the other two bowls.

Albert didn't see it that way, though. He wanted three bowlfuls of cereal, and he wanted to see them all lined up in front of him. It made him feel secure somehow. That way, coming to the end of his first bowlful was not nearly as traumatic, because there was always another. And another. Albert may only have been two but he was already pretty weird.

He had almost finished his first bowl when Emily stumbled up the stairs. He had just noticed that there were not two bowlfuls waiting for him, but only one. He had further observed that Charles had a faint grin on his face and two bowls stacked one inside the other in front of him.

It took Albert about five seconds to put two and two together. Then he fired his spoon at Charles's head. It was the sound of their combined shrieks of rage that met Emily as she stepped into the kitchen.

"What on earth is going on here?"

No one answered. Elizabeth swiveled sideways in her chair and smiled beatifically at her. By this time Albert's face was beet red from failing to breathe between screams. He was trying to swing the hinged tray of the high chair over his head to get out. It would lift about two inches, snap against the vinyl strap that secured it, and come crashing down, shivering his empty bowl and threatening to overturn his dribble glass of juice.

The kettle whistled dementedly on the stove, water sputtering from the spout and sizzling against the red-hot burner. She went to rescue it, setting it on a cool element, where it wheezed down into an exhausted silence.

Charles was busy picking porridge out of his hair. She caught the glint of a smile on his face.

"Charles?"

"I didn't do nothing."

"Anything, Charles. *Anything*." Charles had recently adopted the grammar of his semiliterate friends down the street.

"Did so," said Elizabeth, beaming. "He took the baby's cereal."

By this time the baby, in another bid for freedom, had squirmed down under the anchored tray and wedged there, the vinyl strap taut between his legs. His feet were flailing out in Charles's direction and his head was jammed between the back of the chair and the tray. It didn't seem to hurt his screaming any.

Emily went to rescue him, pausing to cuff Charles on the back of the head on her way by. Her hand came away sticky.

"What's the big idea, Charles? You know how he is about his cereal."

"Don't you hit me. You're not my mother. Ma! Ma!"

"Hit you, Charles? I'll brain you if you don't be quiet."

Albert, his back rigid with rage, had locked himself into position. Working him back up into the seat was like separating the pieces of a Chinese puzzle. The dribble glass bobbed back and forth on its rounded bottom.

"Is there any more cereal?" she asked in desperation.

"Yes," said Elizabeth. "Mom saved some for you."

"Okay. Albert, calm down. I'll get you some more cereal, all right? Just relax." She got another bowl from the cupboard and spooned the cold glop in the bottom of the pot into it. It sat there in a revolting lump.

"Mmmm," she said, plunking the bowl down in front of Albert. "See, Albert. Nice cereal. And there's the other one, right there on the table."

Albert looked from one bowl to the other. He was satisfied. He turned the screams off like a tap.

"Poon," he said. "Poon." She went to get him a spoon.

The bathroom door opened. Mother, her wet hair turbaned with a towel, stepped placidly out, like a visitor from the East.

"Did I hear someone calling?" she asked cheerfully.

After drying her hair, Mrs. Endicott headed off downtown, with the solemn promise that she would be back shortly after noon. This, in rough translation, meant sometime before sundown.

Father was already long gone. He had to be down at the depot early to accept delivery of a shipment of wood they were using to build a stage for the opening day ceremonies.

Emily sat at the kitchen table, sipping tea from her favorite cup, picking idly at the pattern. Albert was busy in the back garden with his truck and a battered spoon from the silverware drawer. Elizabeth and Charles had been wrenched from the television and banished down the block.

138

She kept thinking of that crazy dream, and every time she did her eyes would drift to the calendar above the stove and see that big black "8" staring back at her. She couldn't seem to shake the feeling that something terrible was about to happen. Mother's precious "real world" felt suddenly like little more than a thin layer of tissue stretched taut over another, darker reality. Here and there the tissue had begun to tear away in jagged strips.

Twice she started for the phone, stopped herself, and sat down again. What would she say to Miss Potts? "Well, you see, Miss Potts, I had this dream about Scott Renshaw. Only it wasn't really him. It was this guy, and he looked at me, and I could hear him talking in my head."

Oh, yeah. Sure. That sounded just terrific.

She got out of the chair, walked over to the calendar, and ran the grease pencil back and forth through the 8 until she had utterly obliterated it. Then she marched out the side door, slamming it behind her, and went to check on the children.

Albert was busy loading dirt from the flower beds into the back of his truck. He was loading a few of the flowers along with the dirt, but he was happy, and he was quiet. She let him be, and went to check on Elizabeth and Charles.

There they were, two familiar color patches, playing on a porch down the street. As she turned back to the house she saw someone peering over the edge of the bushes across the street at her. A lean, white face, nodding. Then the breeze took it, turning it into a piece of paper fluttering from the branches.

"Hello. May I speak to Miss Potts, please?"

"May I ask who's calling?"

"Yes, it's Emily Endicott."

"Oh, hello. This is Mrs. Holmes. I'm afraid you

139

can't speak to Miss Potts now, my dear. She's had a bit of an accident.''

"Accident?"

"Oh, nothing too serious, I think. She had a fainting spell this morning. She's in bed resting now. Perhaps you could call back tomorrow.''

"Is there anything I can do?''

"No, I don't think so, dear. Oh, there's my doorbell. That'll be the doctor. I'd better run now. I'll tell Miss Potts you called.''

When Mrs. Holmes opened the door she was met by a tall, strikingly pale figure carrying a doctor's bag.

"Oh, do come in. You must be Dr. Marsh. I am Mrs. Holmes.''

"Yes,'' said the tall gentleman, removing his hat as he stepped into the hall.

"So good of you to come on such short notice. I can't think what can have happened to Dr. Fischer. His secretary said he was called out of town unexpectedly.''

"A death in the family, I believe,'' explained Dr. Marsh.

"Oh, how unfortunate.'' There was something about the doctor's eyes. She found herself staring into them, fascinated. "Are you new to town?'' she heard herself saying.

"Yes, I've only just arrived. I intend on setting up a small practice downtown. It strikes me as a charming little place.''

"Yes, very quiet. Peaceful.'' The doctor turned away from her, looking intently in the direction of the stairs.

"Perhaps I should see the patient now,'' he said.

"Certainly,'' said Mrs. Holmes. "It's just this

way. Up stairs. You can leave your hat there on the table, if you like."

The stairs creaked slightly as she started up them. Halfway up she paused. Behind her there was only silence. She looked back to see what had delayed the doctor. He was directly behind her.

"Oh!" she gasped, startled.

"Is there anything wrong, Mrs. Holmes?"

"No, nothing at all." She refused to meet his glance, starting instead back up the stairs. Outside Miss Potts's door they paused, and she knocked lightly.

"It's just me, Miss Potts," she called. "I've got the doctor with me." She opened the door and they went in.

Miss Potts was lying in the bed, apparently asleep. She did not look well at all. Her color was off, and there were deep hollows about her eyes. As the door closed she appeared to waken.

"Miss Potts," said Mrs. Holmes. "This is Dr. Marsh. He's here to take a look at you."

"Doctor?" said Miss Potts, opening her eyes and squinting in their direction.

"Yes," continued Mrs. Holmes, a little sheepishly. "After this morning the three of us decided that this problem with your health had gone on for too long. You are not well, my dear. If anything were to happen to you, we would all feel just terrible that we hadn't done anything. The doctor's just going to take a quick look at you, aren't you, doctor?"

"Yes, that's all," said the doctor. "Just a quick look."

"Well, I really don't think it's necessary." Miss Potts had struggled to a sitting position and was

141

feeling around the bed table for her glasses. They were not there.

"You haven't seen my glasses, have you, Mrs. Holmes? I can't seem to find them here."

"No," said Mrs. Holmes, looking around the room. "Maybe they're downstairs. I'll go have a look. The doctor would probably prefer to see you in private anyway."

"Thank you, Mrs. Holmes," said the doctor. "That would be best."

As Mrs. Holmes's footsteps faded into the house, the doctor turned slowly to Miss Potts.

"So you've not been feeling well, Miss Potts. Well, we'll just have to see what we can do about that, won't we?"

Mrs. Holmes checked the kitchen and the living room for the missing glasses before she came across them in the dining room. They were sitting folded on the sideboard. She remembered now that they had fallen off when Miss Potts fainted. One of the others must have picked them up and put them there. She headed back upstairs with them.

As she opened the door to reenter the room, she noticed a curious smell in the air. The doctor was just recapping a small bottle of liquid, which he set down on the bedside table next to the water glass.

"Ah, Mrs. Holmes," he said. "I've just given Miss Potts a little something to help her sleep. I can find nothing seriously the matter with her that a few days' rest in bed won't cure. However, she must avoid any excitement whatsoever. Loud noises, bright lights, anything. She's to take the medicine I've left every twelve hours. The instructions are on the bottle. It's rather unpleasant tasting, so she may

142

object. But you must be firm. Can I count on you, Mrs. Holmes?"

"Yes, doctor, certainly. Once every twelve hours."

"Good. And if anything further develops, phone me immediately."

"Yes, I will." The doctor's bag was sitting open on the chair by the bed. Mrs. Holmes had just noticed something protruding from it. Flowers?

The doctor noticed her gaze. He went over and quickly closed the bag, first removing what was in fact a small bouquet of paper flowers.

"Presents for the children," he explained. "It helps to set them more at ease."

With a quick flick of his wrist the flowers disappeared. Mrs. Holmes let out a startled little cry. The doctor extended his hand toward her, and the flowers magically reappeared.

"Please keep them," he said, handing them to her, "with my compliments."

At the front door the doctor paused to put on his hat and gloves. Mrs. Holmes was pleased to see a gentleman still wearing gloves. It put her in mind of the more genteel days of the past.

"Thank you again, doctor, for coming on such short notice."

"No trouble at all," said the doctor, eyeing the darkening sky. "Looks like we have some weather coming on. I'd better be on my way. I've a couple more calls yet. Goodbye, Mrs. Holmes. And remember, no excitement at all."

"Yes, doctor. Thank you. Goodbye." As she closed the door Mrs. Holmes glanced down at her watch. Nearly three o'clock. Miss Blight and Mr. Palmer would be back from shopping any time now. She went to put the kettle on for tea.

Chapter 22

Two rough pieces of plywood had been laid across the beams in the garage. Upon them were stored those battered and broken remnants of the past that his mother could not stand to part with. There was a plastic swimming pool split down one side, a tricycle minus one rear wheel, a sled with twisted runners.

Craig lifted the ladder down from its nail and leaned it against a beam. Climbing it quickly, he retrieved the chamois-wrapped book from the edge of the platform and scampered back down. He set the book on the seat of his bicycle as he returned the ladder to its place on the wall.

His eyes drifted to that far corner of the garage where the tools were hung. Among the familiar shadows there was now another that he could not explain. It looked like a tall figure, standing there studying him.

"Scott, is that you?" He tried to sift the fear from his voice.

There was no answer. The figure remained motionless in the corner. Craig inched backward until he was at the door. With a quick kick he sent it flying open, flooding the corner with light. A wave of relief enveloped him.

Propped against the wall in the corner of the

garage there stood a bundle of branches tied together with ragged strips of cloth. The man next door had given them to mother to stake her bean plants.

Nonetheless, he took it as a sign, and as he drove over to Scott's he was sure that today would be the day they met again.

He waited for two hours in the hole, staring up at the darkened window, convinced somehow that Scott was there, but far too afraid to venture up the fire escape and find out. It was after six when he finally gave up the vigil and climbed up into the lane. He had parked his bike out of sight in an alleyway between a Chinese restaurant and a medical building on the opposite side of the lane. He was on his way to get it when he heard a door slam behind him and the sound of someone starting down a fire escape.

He glanced back and saw Scott, dressed in that faded blue jacket he always wore when he was practicing, and carrying the small black satchel he kept his equipment in. Since the stairs faced the end of the lane, Scott had not caught sight of him yet.

He ducked into the alley and crouched down behind the bike. His mind raced. Where could Scott be going? Why would he have his magic stuff with him?

A little further along the alley a window was open. He could hear the banging of pots and pans, the sounds of people talking, laughing. Overhead there was another sound: the high-pitched wail of a dentist's drill, made all the more shrill and unsettling in the confines of the alley. He felt his stomach tighten as the seconds ticked away and Scott failed to appear.

Maybe he'd left by the other way, through the car lot at the end of the lane. Suddenly he heard the sound of someone approaching the alley entrance. He held his breath and pressed himself against the wall.

An instant later Scott appeared. It must only have taken him a moment to walk by, but it seemed like he stood there framed by the alley walls for an eternity. He was looking down and there was a slight hint of a smile on his face. His lips seemed unnaturally red, and it looked like he had pencilled in his sideburns. His face was as white as the handkerchief peeking from his breast pocket.

Craig waited for a minute or so after he'd passed, trying to get his breath. Then he ventured out into the lane. A voice inside his head was screaming at him, telling him to get on the bike and pedal it just as fast as it could carry him back home.

Instead, he walked slowly to the end of the lane and looked up the street. Scott was standing near the end of the block peering into a store window. As if on cue, he straightened and started walking again. At the corner he turned right and disappeared onto Arlington Avenue.

Craig mounted the bike and started pedaling after him. By the time he reached the corner, Scott was already a fair distance down the street, shuffling quickly along with his head down and the bag swinging by his side. Craig followed, walking the bike now, clinging to the shop side of the street so that he could dart into one of the entranceways if Scott suddenly decided to look back.

They walked for quite a distance, due west through town. The farther they went, the fewer people there were around. Craig felt painfully obvious trailing behind with the bike. He couldn't seem to shake the feeling that this was all just an

146

elaborate game they were playing, that Scott was perfectly aware that he was being followed.

It was beginning to get dark now, and the sky was looking more threatening by the minute. He should have been home long ago. His mother would be sick with worry. But he could no more leave now than he could when he first saw Scott standing by the schoolyard fence last spring. Still the mystery drew him like a magnet, but now he sensed that every step he took was leading him nearest to the truth of it.

It seemed that they had been walking for miles past boarded buildings and run-down restaurants, when suddenly Scott disappeared. One second he was there, and then he was gone and the street was empty. Craig felt panic wash over him. He cautiously approached the last place he'd seen Scott. Tucked between the buildings there was a short laneway opening out into a dead-end street. One short block of squat row houses that ended abruptly in a guard rail and a weathered wooden fence. There was no sign of Scott.

The street seemed strangely silent, the small, dark houses somehow menacing. As he started down it a dog chained to the bumper of a gutted car lunged out at him, barking furiously.

A group of children were playing at the side of the road near the end of the street. There were half a dozen of them huddled by the curb, dropping something down the sewer grating.

Where was Scott? Had he disappeared into one of the houses, or was he simply hiding someplace, waiting to spring out at him and bring the game to an abrupt end?

The children looked up at him suspiciously as he approached with the bike. One of them, a girl of about eight, stood up. She had no shoes on and she wore a faded yellow pinafore. Her hair was a mass of tangles and her frail, thin face was unwashed. None of the others appeared to take any notice of her as she sidestepped them and took several paces in Craig's direction.

Instinctively he stopped, wondering what this strange, almost wild-looking child might want with him. It was little comfort that the bicycle stood between them.

She came no closer than the curb. She simply stood there, fixing him with wide, vacant eyes, and then her arm drifted slowly up from her side and she pointed in the direction of the weathered wooden fence at the end of the street.

He looked, and noticed now that one of the boards had been worked loose at the bottom and swung over to one side. Ample space for someone to squeeze through.

Instantly he understood what she was showing him. He turned back to her, but she had already gone back to join the others. She refused to look up at him as he passed by with the bike.

He chained the bike to the guard rail post and nervously approached the fence. With one last look over his shoulder he squatted down and squeezed through.

It took him a minute to realize where he was. When he did, his heart sank. Scarcely three feet from the fence the ground fell suddenly away, and the Bedford Ravine began. He stood as near to the edge as he dared and looked down into the green dark.

You know what's down there, don't you, dear?

This was the last place in the world he wanted to be right now, but it was far too late to turn back.

Just to his left there was a break in the bushes that covered the embankment, and the grass gave way to bare ground where a path had been worn. He pushed through the bushes and started hesitantly down the path, grasping frantically for branches to slow his descent on the steep hill. The rich, alien smell of the ravine rushed up to meet him, and he felt his mouth go dry.

The ground at the bottom was spongy with leaf mold and moisture. The thick canopy of trees allowed only scattered shafts of light to sift through. Squirrels darted noisily through the undergrowth. Every sound seemed eerily magnified. He waded cautiously forward through the thick tangle of creepers, pausing every now and then to listen.

Everywhere there were traces of earlier intruders: a shopping cart wedged between tree trunks halfway down a hill, a bundle of handbills bloated with moisture, a shoe half-buried in the silt of the stream that ran through the ravine, the remnants of fires, forts.

But still there was no sign of Scott. In the growing dimness shadows took shape. He moved nervously along the bank of the stream, following it until it ducked beneath the grating of a storm sewer pipe and disappeared.

He was near the western edge of the ravine now. Directly ahead of him loomed the old wooden trestle. It looked in the twilight like some strange web spun between the trees. Nestled close by it on the crest of the hill above him stood the Caledon Depot.

The face of the hill itself was bare, the soil eroded into ancient channels where the rain washed down. At the foot of the hill there was a tangle of railroad ties, like huge pickup sticks abandoned in the under-growth. An old baggage cart lay upended nearby.

Perched on one of the rusted wheels was a large black bird. It may only have been a trick of the light, but the bird's eyes appeared to glow. Craig stood there motionless, terrified that it might fly at him if he moved. But the bird did not stir. It just sat there watching him with its luminous red eyes. Then, suddenly, with a terrific beating of wings, it took to the air. It circled for a time above the trees, then came to rest on the roof of the depot.

At that instant the lights came on.

Chapter 23

It was after five before mother returned. She dropped two stuffed shopping bags onto the couch and collapsed between them, kicking off her high heels.

"Oh, my aching feet," she moaned. "Sorry I'm late, love. Have you heard from your father yet?"

"No. Nothing."

"That man. He promised me he'd be home for dinner tonight. Did you remember to take the hamburger meat out of the freezer?"

"Yes. Say, mom, you don't think dad's still down at the depot, do you?"

"Where else? He practically lives there these days, doesn't he? How have the kids been?"

"Fine. Elizabeth and Charles are on the Puccis' porch playing Monopoly. Albert's in his room." The dull feeling of dread she'd managed to keep in check for most of the day suddenly swept over her again. She went to the front window. It was already beginning to get dark.

"Storm coming," said mother. She stood up, braced her hands in the small of her back, and stretched. "I'll just go and peek in on Albert.

"Albert, honey," she trilled, as she padded through the kitchen in her stockinged feet. "Look who's ho-o-ome."

At seven o'clock there was still no sign of Mr. Endicott, and it had started to rain. The hamburger patties that had been left warming in the oven for the past half hour were looking pretty disgusting by this point. They had shrunk to almost half their original size and sat there pathetically in tiny puddles of grease. A thin yellow crust had formed over the bowl of mashed potatoes sitting beside them on the rack.

The children, faint with hunger, stood with their faces pasted to the front window, listening for the hiss of approaching cars on the wet road.

Mother vascillated between anger and growing concern. She fanned through the front section of the paper for the third time, her eyes wandering every few minutes to the clock above the fridge.

"Well, I suppose we'd better sit down and eat," she announced at seven fifteen. "Before everything is completely ruined."

It was a little late for that. Nobody complained, though, as they quickly downed the meal in silence. Directly after dinner mother started phoning around to some of the other members of the historical society, asking if they'd heard anything from father. Mr. Andrews said that he'd been over at the depot that afternoon with father. He'd left around four. Father was just finishing up some painting and had said he'd be leaving shortly as well. Mr. Andrews didn't know what could be keeping him.

Mother was just hanging up the receiver when Emily came clumping up the basement stairs. She was wearing a large yellow rain poncho and a pair of Mr. Endicott's rubber boots. An old camping flashlight was clutched in her hand.

"I'm going to look for him," she announced. "I can't stand sitting around waiting anymore."

Mother took one look at her. She knew it would be useless to argue.

"He'll be at the depot."

"I know."

"I swear I'm going to murder that man when he gets home."

"Don't worry, mom. You know dad. He's just gotten involved in something and lost track of the time. Everything will be all right." She opened the door and stepped out into the alley. "I think I'll take the bike. It's not raining that hard, and it'll be a lot faster. Dad can put it in the trunk on the drive back."

"Emily," mother called out as she reached the back gate. She turned to face her. "Be careful."

The bike was propped against the back wall of the house beside the laundry stoop. It was an old delivery bike with a large metal basket welded right onto it for carrying orders. The tires were thick and the frame weighed a ton. They didn't bother locking it up because no one in their right mind would bother stealing it.

Emily walked the bike down the alley and out to the curb. As she got on she turned and waved to Albert, who was standing watching at the front window. He didn't wave back. He just stood there, solemnly sucking his thumb, as she rode off into the rain.

The trip, which would normally have taken ten minutes, took nearly half an hour in the rain. She had wedged the flashlight between the bars of the delivery basket and switched it on. The beam of light bounced ahead of her on the slick road. She

153

kept her eyes fixed on it, ignoring the pelting of the rain against her face.

By the time she made the turn onto Bedford Road the light was already beginning to dim. The dark seemed thicker here somehow, pressing against her face like musty fabric. As she neared the bridge over the ravine she got off the bike. Her imagination wanted to people the shadows with faces. She walked quickly, concentrating on the light, keeping to the curb edge of the sidewalk as she crossed the bridge.

There was no sign of the car. As she neared the path she had taken that day with Albert, she looked out over the moving sea of grass toward the depot. Light spilled from the waiting room windows.

She could still see him standing there at the foot of the stairs with the strange look on his face.

'Cared! 'Cared, Emmy!

"Believe me, Albert," she whispered, laying the bike down in the grass. "I'm scared too."

More than once as she picked her way along the tenuous path she stopped, suddenly whirled around, and panned the flashlight out over the grass, convinced that someone was there.

The field felt as if it had come to life, hissing menacingly in her ear, reaching out with wet, green arms to grasp her.

At last she scrambled up onto the platform and the safety of the porch. Propped against the wall by the door there was an old broom from back home, beside it a bag of garbage. The door was open a touch.

Emily sloughed off the wet poncho and wiped her face on her arm. Free of the field, the crazy fear she had felt before had edged aside a little. She strode boldly over to the door.

154

"Dad, it's me," she called as she stepped inside. "Boy, are you going to—"

She felt a tingling run straight through her like an electric shock. A small, thin figure stood facing her at the end of the hall. A little girl, a finger pressed to her lips.

"Shhh," she whispered. "The show's begun."

Chapter 24

It was raining, raining furiously. Miss Potts's feet sank down into the deep mud of the field. Her clothes were slicked to her skin, and her loose hair hung in dripping tendrils round her head. Behind her the wind stood, slamming the gate and blowing her deeper into the field.

In no time at all she had lost all sense of direction. The thick sea of grass arched over her, its dry, rasping voice filled her head. Panicked, she pushed on blindly, knowing that she must get to the depot before it was too late.

Midway across the field she suddenly came into a clearing, a bowl-shaped hollow where the grass had been beaten flat. On the far side of the clearing she could hear someone moving in the grass. The rain against her seemed to freeze. She felt enshrouded in ice, unable to move.

A tall dark figure detached itself from the grass and stumbled down the side of the hill toward her. It was almost upon her before she recognized the rain-slicked features of the face. It was Mr. Palmer.

"Hello, Miss Potts," he said quite matter-of-factly.

"Mr. Palmer. What on earth are you doing here?"

"I came to help," he said. She could hardly hear

him over the hissing of the grass. For the first time she noticed that he was carrying something. His eyes followed her.

"I found her," he said. "Over there, at the depot."

Miss Potts slopped through the pool of water that had gathered in the hollow. It was Emily in his arms.

"She shouldn't have been there," he went on. "No place for a young girl to be hanging about."

He held the limp body out to her like a bunch of roses he'd just snipped from the garden. The smile on his face was full of pride and pleasure. Rainwater spilled from his mouth like water from the rim of an overflowing bucket. She watched it sheeting down his chin as he transferred the weight from his arms to her own.

The girl moaned. Her face was covered in mud. Miss Potts felt the reassuring swell of breath against her hands.

"We'd better get her home," she said, and then saw that Mr. Palmer had turned away and was walking back into the grass. Already she could hardly see him through the rain.

"Wait," she cried. "Don't go back there." But he had disappeared into the grass.

She was within sight of the fence, and safety, when the wet grass seemed to spring shut on her ankle like a trap. She stumbled, dropping the girl like a rag doll into the grass. As she bent close to the thin, muddied face, Emily moaned slightly.

Miss Potts tore up a handful of wet grass and tried to clear the mud from the girl's eyes and mouth. She used her fingers to feel in the dark, wiping with the grass, feeling, then wiping again. And suddenly she had the terrifying sensation that part of the face had come away in her hand, leaving broken soil and tangled roots of grass in its wake.

It lasted just an instant, and then the face was whole again. But as she bent to pick up the slack body, her heart was racing. Then finally they were free of the field, and she felt the cool perfumed air of the garden in her face.

A dim bulb glowed above the back stoop. She hurried over the clipped damp grass toward it. Rain chanelled down the gutter spout, emptying into a battered tin tub beneath it. She headed down the dark alley leading to the front of the house.

Emily seemed to be breathing more easily now. Her shoes dragged along the brick as Miss Potts struggled down the narrow passageway. Dark clods of soil speared with long grass, dropped to the concrete in their wake.

At the front door, as she fumbled with her keys, the screen door swung shut against them with a sudden gust of wind. A muddy lump of turf fell root-end up on the coco matting, the soil spilling away from long filaments of grass.

She closed the door behind her and hurried across the darkened hall, pausing to rest the girl on her lap at the foot of the stairs before starting up to her room. Once there, she lay Emily down on the bed, put a pillow under her head, and ran to get a blanket from the linen closet in the hall.

Everything would be all right now, she told herself as she headed back to the room. There was nothing in the house to harm them.

She walked through the door and glanced over at the bed. The blanket fell from her hand. There on the bed, one end propped up on her pillow, lay a tangled mass of mud and grass.

* * *

Miss Potts sprang up in the bed. Her face was bathed in sweat and her heart was hammering in her chest. She felt beside her in the bed, dreading that the muddy mass from her dream might be lying there next to her. There was nothing.

She had no idea what time it was, but the darkness of the room disturbed her. She switched on her bedside lamp and put on her glasses. It was then she saw the small vial of liquid on the table, and confused memories of that morning started to slowly return. A doctor had been to see her. He had given her something he said would make her sleep. Try though she might, she could not remember his face. Only the hypnotic drone of his voice and those dark eyes boring into her.

A sudden panic seized her. She jumped from the bed. The time! She had to know the time! The clock was hidden away in her dresser drawer, where its infernal ticking could not drive her crazy. She flung open the drawer. There it lay upon a bed of cotton briefs and faded camisoles. She stared down at it in disbelief.

It was nine o'clock. She had slept through the entire day. With a sick sensation of dread she rushed across the room to the window. She reached up over the window seat and flung open the drapes.

Chapter 25

The Children's Show

IV

The magician sauntered to the edge of the stage, shaking the paper cone. Roses spilled from the end of it onto the skirt of the stage and down into the audience, more roses than the cone could possibly have contained. With a flick of the hand he tossed it suddenly into the air. It fluttered open, showering candies and small souvenirs upon the children gathered near the stage. They scrambled after them, squealing delightedly as they snatched them up.

"Well, well," said the magician, shielding his eyes with his hand as he glanced out into the audience. "I can see some familiar faces in the crowd tonight, but I believe I also see some new faces. It's always nice to see new faces. Yes, you by the door. Do come in, dear. Don't be shy. There's much more yet to come."

The girl edged uncertainly into the room. There was something wrong, something terribly wrong, but she didn't know what it was. Confused, she looked back at the door, and the small girl standing there, her arm full of programs. She had the strange

160

feeling that if she reached out and touched the girl her hand would go straight through.

The magician continued. "I see that many of you out there already have a copy of our little book. But for those of you who do not yet have one and who would like to become a part of the professor's magical society, there will be ample opportunity during the course of the performance to participate."

The girl made her way across the dim room and sat on the floor at the back of the group. Some faces, white with light, twisted around to see her. The smell of the flowers was almost sickening.

"Now, for our next trick I will require the assistance of someone from the audience. Are there any volunteers?" Hands shot up into the air, waving wildly. The magician nodded to a boy near the front who immediately bounced up and scampered onto the stage.

"This trick is called Cups and Balls. It is a very old illusion, practiced by the court magicians of ancient Egypt and China. Here are three cups, empty as you can see. I will place them upside down on the table. And under this one, in the middle, I will place this ball. Now, young man, watch very closely."

The magician proceeded to shift the position of the cups on the table with dizzying speed. Occasionally he would stop and ask the boy which cup contained the ball. But the boy would always guess wrong. Sometimes it did not appear to be under any of the cups, at other times it seemed to be under all three. The trick concluded with the ball, apparently vanished, being plucked from the amazed boy's mouth, to the delight of the crowd.

161

The performance continued. There were tricks with cards and coins and linking rings. A shawl, dropped to the floor, revealed a large glass bowl of fish when removed. Yards of knotted silk were drawn from the magician's mouth. A small bottle poured cup after cup of whatever the children wished, but was never emptied.

Every now and then the girl in the back would wonder in a lazy sort of way how she happened to come here, and then the magician's eyes would meet hers and the thought would drift off like the candle smoke curling into the air above the stage, and there would be only the magic again.

"And now I wonder if there might be a young lady in the audience willing to come up and assist the professor in a charming little illusion entitled the Vanishing Lady."

A couple of hands went up at the front, but the magician ignored them. He had fixed his eyes on the girl at the back. They were the gentle eyes of an all-loving father. They flowed into her, exploring every corner and crevice of her, quieting all doubt.

Now, now my dear. There's nothing to fear, nothing at all.

The words sounded inside her, like music. It was all she could do to stop her hand from flying up from her side. And yet there was something, something just out of reach.

She pulled her eyes from the magician's and willed her hands down to the floor. One of them came to rest in a small puddle of water.

The magician turned from her and gestured to another girl near the stage. She went up to join him.

"Now, to assure you that there are no hidden trap doors or other devices, I will lay this sheet of newspaper down upon the stage. And upon the paper

162

*I will place this chair. A perfectly ordinary chair,
as you can see. . . ."*

*Water? The girl glanced out through the tall
windows on the wall of the room opposite her. The
sky was clear. A full moon silvered the floor beneath
the windows. But now, wound in with the magician's
words, she thought she heard the muted rumble of
thunder in the distance and the patter of rain on the
roof.*

*"Now, dear, would you sit down in the chair for
me? Yes, that's a girl. Not nervous, are you? That's
good.*

*"I'm now going to take this sheet and drape it
over the chair and its occupant. Like so. And now,
before your very eyes, I will make the young lady—
vanish."*

*As he said the final word he whisked the sheet
away. The girl was gone.*

*The audience gasped in amazement, then broke
into thunderous applause. The magician bowed
politely and pointed down into the crowd.*

*"And a nice hand for the young lady," he said.
For there, sitting quietly in their midst, was the
vanished girl.*

*As the performance continued the girl at the back
of the room purposely averted her eyes from the
magician's, fixing her attention instead on the
children in the audience. There was something about
them that troubled her. They reminded her of dolls,
with stitched-on smiles and wide, empty eyes. She
felt that if she shook them their heads would fall
limply forward onto their chests.*

*The sound of the rain was stronger now,
drumming almost urgently on the roof like countless
tiny fists.*

Suddenly a hush fell over the room. The children

163

in the audience stared silently at one another as though anticipating what was to come. The magician cleared away the props he had been using, and wheeled a bare table to the center of the stage.

"And now," he said, walking to the edge of the platform, "we come to the highlight of the evening's entertainment, the Decollation, an illusion so astonishing you will not believe your eyes. Do I have a volunteer?"

Immediately a fat boy at the front of the room raised his hand, waving it wildly in the air. He held his head strangely, awkwardly pitched to one side. From the back of the room the girl watched him, and a memory stirred inside her, almost within reach.

The magician ignored the boy at the front, nodding instead to another boy on the other side of the stage. As the fat boy brought his arm down his hand drifted slowly to his neck and his fingers fanned across it.

In one terrifying instant reality knifed through the illusion.

Freddie. Fat Freddie! Miss Potts's words suddenly sounded in her head.

There was an ugly red welt around his neck, and now and then Freddie would reach up and run his fingers along it.

"Now let's have a nice round of applause for the young gentleman," said the professor. He extended his hand and helped the volunteer up the last stair and onto the stage. As the boy turned to face the audience Emily gasped.

It was Craig Chandler.

"Shh," said someone beside her.

"Reality and illusion," said the magician, guiding the boy over to the table, "which is which? Could

164

Could it be, dear children, that life and death them-
selves are no more than illusions? Could it be
that? . . ."

But do you know what I think? I think he died up
there on stage that night.

"No!" screamed Emily, jumping to her feet. The
word echoed through the room like thunder.

For an instant everything appeared to freeze in
time: the magician's hands fixed in the act of
draping the cloth over the boy, the candle flames
like tongues of ice atop the wicks, the children
turned to stone.

Then the professor's hands dropped to his side
and he turned to face her, fixing her with those
incredible eyes. In them she read surprise, disap-
pointment, but just below the surface something else,
something that made her veins freeze. She could feel
them tunneling into her, smashing the lights of
thought, like father stumbling into the basement
bulb.

But when he spoke, the words were gentle,
measured, the tone that of a patient parent indulging
a troublesome child.

"Well, well," he said. "It seems that someone
has something to say. What is it, my dear? Come,
come now. Don't be shy. Speak up."

The others in the audience had craned their heads
around to observe her. They all had the same dazed
look in their eyes.

"Perhaps the young lady feels left out,"
continued the magician. "Perhaps she would like to
participate in the illusion. Is that it, my child?"

But below the surface of the soothing words
another voice, cold, bloodless, sounded inside her.

Look at me. I said, look at me, girl.

Confusion had already begun to enshroud her.

165

She had forgotten why she'd stood up in the first place. Her eyes locked onto his.

The silence of the room had begun crack. Whispers broke in several places as child turned to child. She tried to tear her eyes away, tried to anchor her thoughts to something, struggled to reopen the door that she felt had just swung shut inside.

"Come along, my dear. The others are impatient for the performance to continue." And beneath that gentle voice, the other.

Come here—now!

Her feet began to move of their own will toward the stage.

"Now let's have a nice hand for the young lady," said the professor. The children shifted aside to let her past, clapping heartily and peering up at her with broad, empty grins.

No! No! Some small distant part of her screamed out, but she moved steadily forward, now up the stairs to the stage. It was awkward because of the boots she was wearing.

Boots? Yes, it had been raining, raining hard. I was on the bike, yes, going somewhere. Where?

There was a sudden flash, and the room was filled with white light. She looked up at the magician's face, and in the instant before the light vanished saw quite another person standing there, extending his hand to her.

The toe of the big boots caught on the edge of the top stair. Pain knifed up her leg as she lurched helplessly forward. Then the floor rushed up to meet her, and the room went dark.

When she opened her eyes again, she found herself lying on the floor of her room. The side of her face itched from the touch of the woolen rug against it.

She was staring into the shadows under the bed, vaguely wondering if what she had just seen skittering out of sight was another centipede, but feeling far too detached from this body lying on the floor to feel anything like fear.

She couldn't remember how she had gotten there. Her eyes burned and the inside of her head felt like someone had packed it with hot cloths. There was a dull throb of pain in her leg.

A glass with a thermometer in it sat on the table by the bed, beside it a small bottle of pills. Air bubbles beaded the inside of the glass and clung to the thermometer like buds on a branch. Overhead she heard the muted drone of the television. The cellar door opened, and someone started down.

She listened absently to the familiar creaking of the stairs, the swish of slippered feet across the concrete floor, the snap of the pull chain as the light above the workbench was switched on.

The door opened. And her mother walked in.

"Emily," she cried, dropping the quilt she was carrying. "Are you hurt? Did you fall out of bed?" She knelt down beside her. "Here, let me help you up."

Emily put her arm around her and felt herself being lifted effortlessly up onto the bed. That perfume her mother was wearing. Very strong. What was it? Roses, yes, roses.

"I feel funny. Cold," she said.

"It's the fever, love. You've been a very sick young lady. Had us all worried to death. The worst is over now though. The doctor says you'll be up and around in a few days. Here, I've brought you a nice warm blanket. We'll just tuck you in all nice

167

and comfy and you can have a little sleep. How does that sound?''

As her mother leaned over to help ease her down onto the pillow Emily caught another fleeting whiff of her perfume. But there was something else now. A sharp, musty smell, the smell of books in damp basements. The dark smell of mildew and mold. And then it was gone.

''Is there something wrong, dear?'' *She had the sudden strange feeling that the room and everything in it were only pictures painted on a screen. If she could just catch hold of the edge and—*

''Lie down, Emily.'' *A crack had appeared in the comforting. The voice momentarily bristled, the hand tightened on her shoulder, urging her down. She slumped back in the bed, peering up into her mother's face, pale with powder. The eyes caught her, held her. Cold, piercing eyes, pinning her to the bed like a butterfly to a board. A voice droned in her head.*

Just a little sleep, a little sleep, no pain, just a little . . .

She felt so cold, so terribly cold. Mother slowly drew the quilt up over her chest.

Suddenly there was a banging at the door. Loud, urgent. She shot up in the bed.

''What was that?''

''It's nothing, dear. Just Albert with his truck.''

'Cared. 'Cared!

''Now lie down.''

She lay back and looked into her mother's eyes. They seemed to be drawing her into them. She felt herself teetering on the edge of an abyss.

No pain, just a little sleep, just . . .

Drifting, drifting, panic quickly fading into peace. She felt cold, so cold. If only she could sleep, just

168

a little sleep. The quilt settled gently over her face.
Somewhere she could hear someone shouting her
name. She opened her eyes, confused, suddenly
afraid.

. . . a little sleep, no . . .
Something cold touched her neck.
. . . pain.
There was a loud crash, the sound of shattering
glass. Thunder echoed through the room, and with
it another sound, a high, furious howl of frustration
and defeat.

"Emily. Emily."

She sat up slowly, pushing off the musty sheet
spread over her. It was dark. She was in the depot.
Miss Potts stood in the shattered window, shining a
flashlight into the room. Drop sheets covered the
floor. Papers, cans of paint strewn everywhere.

Miss Potts scrambled through the window,
fanning the light over the room.

"Are you all right, my dear?"

"Yes," said Emily, climbing down from the half-
constructed stage she had found herself lying on. "I
think so."

They heard a moan. It seemed to come within the
stage. Although the framing was finished, the boards
that formed the platform had not yet all been nailed
in place. There was a large hole, partially covered
by loose planks. The sound came from inside the
hole.

They stepped through sawdust and board ends,
and Miss Potts shone the flashlight down inside.

Two figures lay there motionless, locked in one
another's arms. As the light struck them one of them
stirred and broke free of the other's grasp. He rolled

over onto the floor and his eyes fluttered open. It was Craig Chandler.

Beside him on the floor lay another boy. For an instant the three of them were staring down into the wide, startled eyes of Scott Renshaw. But even as they looked, the body seemed to flicker slightly, like a candle flame. For a time it appeared luminous, almost transparent. And then all at once it crumbled inwards, like the spent ashes of a settling fire.

On the floor of the depot, in its place, lay the tangled branches of a rose bush, bristling with thorns. And scattered on the boards beneath it, a drift of pale red petals.

Chapter 26

"And so," concluded Mr. Endicott, "it is with great pleasure that I officially announce the opening of the Caledon Railway Museum."

There was heartfelt applause throughout the room as he hurriedly collected his looseleaf sheets and fled the podium. Emily, seated with mother and the rest of the brood in the front row, clapped vigorously, not the least reason being that this was the last time she would have to listen to the speech. For the past week father had spent half his time stationed outside her room, reciting it to the lightbulb above the workbench. She knew it word for word.

Albert sat almost unrecognizable beside her, his hair slicked back off his face, his skin scrubbed several shades lighter than usual. He was wearing a white suit with short pants and knee socks. His shoes shone. He looked like he had been carefully clipped from a British magazine.

Mother had stationed herself strategically between an immaculate Elizabeth and Charles. She wore that fixed, unflagging smile she saved for such occasions.

Emily winked at father as he shuffled past on his way to the refuge of his chair. Mother smiled benignly through him, her eyes focused on some invisible object in the distance.

Next the mayor took the podium. While he

rambled on interminably, Emily let her attention wander around the room. The turnout was surprisingly good, especially for a holiday weekend. She counted forty-four.

In the second row from the last she spotted Miss Potts, who was seated between Mr. Palmer and Mrs. Holmes. She too was looking around the room. Their eyes met and they traded smiles.

By the end of the speech Albert was squirming relentlessly because of the of the suit and the sight of a model engine in a nearby display case. Now and then, mother would lean over, smiling, and whisper some dire warning in his ear.

Finally the mayor was finished. People were invited to stay for wine and cheese, and to view the results of the work to date. A couple of the men from the historical society folded the chairs and stacked them against the wall. Someone in uniform served drinks from a portable bar that had been rolled in front of the stage.

Soon people were milling about, clutching cigarettes and plastic cups of wine. The room filled rapidly with smoke and noise.

Emily, with Albert in tow, wandered off to find Miss Potts. They discovered her standing alone by the stairwell that led to the second floor. There was a chain strung between the iron rails with a sign suspended from it, reading Danger. Do Not Enter. Stacked behind the stairs were cans of paint and folded tarpaulins. Miss Potts was leaning over the chain, peering up into the dark.

Albert raced over to her and flung his arms around her legs. Miss Potts jumped and let out a startled cry.

"Oh, it's you, Albert. You nearly frightened me to death. My, don't you look handsome tonight."

172

Albert made a face. "'Tairs," he said suddenly, quite seriously, and went over to peek tentatively under the chain.

"Hi, Miss Potts," said Emily. "I'm sorry if Albert frightened you. I'm afraid he's a little stir crazy right now."

"That's quite all right, my dear. These sorts of things make me a little stir crazy myself, to tell you the truth. I notice Craig didn't come. I was hoping he'd be here."

"No, I asked him about it again today when I was over there, but he says he's still not ready. It's hard enough getting him to walk down the street right now. He's still not convinced that Scott's gone."

"It will take time," said Miss Potts. "But he has plenty of that, thanks to you."

"No!" yelled Albert. He was hanging onto the chain at the foot of the stairs, shaking it for all he was worth. "No 'tairs," he said. "No!"

"He's overtired," said Emily. "He gets like this." She went over and knelt down beside him. She pointed across the room to where father's layout was set up. A crowd had gathered round it to watch the trains thread the intricate maze of track. Elizabeth and Charles stood beside him at the controls; mother looked on over his shoulder.

"Why don't you go over there and see the trains with mommy?" Emily said. Albert scanned the crowd suspiciously, then spotted the family. He dashed across the room to join them.

"Tains!" he squealed. "Tains!"

Miss Potts was rooting through her bag when Emily rejoined her. "Here," she said, taking out a foil-wrapped package and handing it to Emily. "A present from Mrs. Holmes. Brownies, I believe. You'll think twice before you compliment her on her

173

baking again." She continued rummaging through the bag. "I've something here to show you, if I can just find it. I went back to the library yesterday. I wanted to look through those back issues of the paper again. Ah, here."

She brought out a folded sheet of photocopying and handed it to Emily. "Take a look at this," she said. "I found it in the Monday, August 10, issue of the paper. I don't know how we missed it before, though I suspect that Scott Renshaw's presence in the library at the time may have had something to do with it."

Emily unfolded the sheet. The headline stood out immediately:

GIRL STILL MISSING

Police are still searching for the whereabouts of a thirteen-year-old Caledon girl who disappeared last Saturday evening. The girl was last seen in the vicinity of the railroad depot. The depot, closed since a recent fire gutted the second floor, appears to have been broken into over the weekend.

Neighbors reported hearing noises and seeing lights inside the building on Saturday night, but a thorough search of the premises by police has failed to turn up any trace of the missing girl. Yesterday searchers combed the dense brush of the Bedford Ravine without success.

The girl is described as being about five feet tall, of medium build, with short dark hair and glasses. At the time of her disappearance she was wearing white cotton pants and a blue sweater. Anyone who may have any information on the missing girl is urged to contact the Caledon Police Department immediately.

"I went through the paper for the rest of 1964," said Miss Potts when Emily had finished reading. "The girl was never found. It was as if she vanished into thin air."

"She did," said Emily, folding the sheet and handing it back to Miss Potts. She was staring fixedly over at the empty stage. "I saw her—that night at the show. She was the girl he used for the Vanishing Lady trick.

"It all makes sense in an awful sort of way, doesn't it? Fat Freddie volunteered for the Decollation trick and died later of a broken neck. This girl volunteered for the Vanishing Lady illusion and then disappeared."

"Come," said Miss Potts. "Let's walk." She took Emily's arm, and the two of them ambled slowly around the edge of the room, where display cases had been stationed at intervals against the wall. In one a lump of ancient sod sat in a wooden box inlaid with satin. It was a piece of the first spadeful of soil turned in the construction of the Niagara Northwestern. Alongside it were pictures of the day the first train had come to town, with crowds gathered on the platform in their finery, the depot decked out in bunting.

"Now I know why Craig couldn t come," said Emily. "It's as if beneath all this, just out of sight, out of reach, the show is still here. I can still feel it."

"Yes," said Miss Potts. "When you and Albert came upon me by the stairs I had just sensed it too. There was a sudden smell of roses in the air, and for an instant I was certain I saw the magician,

175

standing there in the shadows at the top of the stairs. It will pass. We, too, need time.''

They paused before another case. Here there were ticket stubs, old timetables, faded posters urging farm hands to travel west and help harvest the crops, a placard cautioning young ladies who were traveling alone. And in the midst of these, an old, crumbling playbill for a magic show.

Their eyes settled on it, and for a time they were silent, each alone with her own thoughts. It was Emily who spoke first.

''Miss Potts?''

''Yes, my dear.''

''It doesn't seem real, any of it. It was like a dream we had.''

''Yes, I know. But it was real, all too real. The danger is that we begin to believe it *was* a dream.''

''He will be back, won't he?''

''Yes,'' said Miss Potts ''I believe he will be back. A darker magic has left its mark forever on this place, I fear. And when that night comes round again it will play itself out as before. There will be one or two new faces in the crowd, of course. He will see to that, for he is always anxious to see new faces, always eager for others to step onstage with him and claim the prize. But the show itself will never change; it is fixed forever as it was on that first night.''

''And Scott Renshaw?''

''He too will be back, though next time surely with another name, perhaps even another face. He cannot help but be back, you see, for he is simply the magician in another guise. He is the Pied Piper, the peddler of wonder, leading the children into the dark. He is the seductive stranger in the schoolyard, the boy pasting magic to the poles.

176

"This time he was thwarted. Next time we may not be so lucky. All we can do is wait, and watch, and trust that when the night draws near again, there will be someone left who remembers the last time, and is ready for him."

"Someone like me," said Emily, as she watched their twin reflections in the glass of the case. And there was not a trace of fear in her voice.

Miss Potts's hand alighted gently on her arm.

"Yes, my dear," she said. "Someone like you."

Epilogue

It was some time near the end of September before Craig finally felt strong enough to confront the ghost.

His mother was in the backyard putting a fresh coat of paint on the fence when he went to get the bike from the garage.

"Thought I'd go for a little ride," he said. "Need anything at the store?"

"Not that I can think of. Oh, be careful. Don't touch anything. It's all wet." She held open the gate with green fingers and let him through into the lane.

"Be back in a bit," he said. As he neared the end of the lane he stopped to make sure he had the book in his bag.

The front tire was soft. He pedaled close to the curb, skirting the storm drains, weaving the bulging rubber around bits of broken glass. Every person he passed wore Scott's face.

He stopped at the first service station he saw to get some air. While the bell dinged sluggishly and the tire hardened he felt a shadow fall over him. Ghost fingers gripped his shoulder. He whirled around.

An attendant stood there, wiping grease from his hands with a rag.

"Hey, take it easy kid," he said, smiling. "Just

be sure you hang up that hose when you're done, you hear?"

Craig nodded and turned back to the bike.

As the boy drove off the attendant glanced up from the car he was servicing at the pump and shook his head. He'd never seen anyone look quite that frightened before.

The route was so familiar he could have done it in his sleep. Soon he was bumping down the rutted lane on the bike. He stopped at the foot of the fire escape and got off. His legs felt limp, as though they might buckle beneath him. He took the book from the saddle bag and slipped it under his shirt.

The rail felt slack and sticky in his hand as he started up the stairs. The whole structure seemed to sway beneath him like the web of some immense spider hidden on the rooftops just out of sight. Looking down, the glass-and-brick-strewn ground seemed miles away. By the time he got to the top his heart was hammering furiously in his chest.

The breezeway was deserted, doors shut, drapes drawn. Only the umbrella clothesline remained, looking like some bizarre metal scarecrow keeping the pigeons at bay. The soft planks were spotted with their droppings. Four of the dull fat birds waddled to the edge of the flat roof and peered vacantly down at him out of the sides of their heads, their necks shimmering emerald in the late afternoon light.

He stopped in front of the door. Instead of the curtains that had been there before, there was yellowed newspaper taped over the window: "Mid-Winter Clearout!" "Spy Reports Probed," "More Five-Minute Ideas for Cooked Carrots," "Four Die in Fire."

179

Beneath the last there was photo. Brittle yellow flames spewed from a second-story window. The building was festooned with ice from the fire hoses trained upon the blaze.

He had to stop himself from knocking, convinced that if he did there would be a quick scurry of footsteps, the door would swing open, and Scott would be standing there smiling at him as though nothing at all had happened.

On the rooftop he could hear the pigeons pacing through the gravel, cooing to themselves. He turned and walked the length of the apartment along the breezeway, trying to get a glimpse inside. But all he saw were the sun-bleached backs of drapes, dead flies on the sills, brown rings where potted plants had once sat.

He stopped. In the last window there was a small metal cup with a withered rose standing in it. The side of the cup was elaborately tooled with hieroglyphs. He recognized it instantly as Scott's. It was one of the set he used in the Cups and Balls routine.

He backed away from the window, bumping into the clothesline, sending its laced metal arms in a shrill swing. The pigeons lifted off from the roof, the sound of their wings snapping in the still air like the clapping of hands.

He swung around quickly, in time to see a corner of the drape stir. Or was it simply the reflection of wings on the window? Two petals from the rose fluttered down to the dirty sill.

He walked back to the door, staring down through the cracks between the planks, suddenly feeling that the dark beneath was bottomless, the whole building set adrift in the void. Blood thundered in his head.

There was no choice now. He had to know. The handle seemed to almost turn itself in his hand.

There was a soft click and the door swung open, banging up against the wall. For a moment he stood there paralyzed, and then he walked in.

The room was in ruins. Great hunks of plaster hung from the walls or lay in heaps on the floor. The lathing beneath looked like bone. The floor was strewn with papers, pieces of charred clothing. A blackened mattress leaned against a wall.

Somehow it came as no surprise. This was the real room, the room he had seen in the mirror once. The other one, Scott's room, had never really existed. It had all been only an elaborate illusion.

There was a tattered woolen blanket tacked to the window. Light spilled through two holes in it like the beams from a projectionist's booth. He made his way across the room to the door and the rest of the apartment.

He had never been through this door before. As he opened it now he saw stretching before him a long, narrow hall. Several doors led off the hall on the breezeway side of the building. At the far end was the front door.

"Hello? Is there anyone there?" he called. His voice sounded hollow, bouncing off the bare, scarred walls.

The rooms were empty, the floors thick with dust and droppings. The walls were covered in crayon scrawl. He kept thinking he would walk through one of them and run head-on into the shoeless girl with the yellow pinafore who had pointed him down into the ravine that night. He could picture her standing there clutching a crayon in her hand and staring up at him emptily.

He entered the last room, at the far end of the hall. Through the thin curtains that covered the window he could see the outline of the cup on the sill and the dry flower inside it.

The floor of this room was littered with leaves. A window must have been left open, allowing them to blow in. As he crossed the room to the window they crackled noisily underfoot.

He lifted the edge of the curtain. There was a sudden, unmistakable scent of roses in the air. Resting in the cup, where the dry and faded flower had been before, there stood a freshly cut rose.

Behind him something fell to the floor with a crash. He whirled around. An old card table like the one Scott had used when he practiced must have been leaning against the wall behind the door. For some reason it had fallen over, pushing the door almost closed in the process.

Slashed in crayon on the wall above it were the words *Welcome, Craig.*

Mild laughter seemed to titter through the room. In utter terror he ran, racing down the hall, fully expecting Scott to step through one of the open doorways in his path.

He reached the bedroom and slammed the door shut. For a long time he stood there with his back wedged against it, his senses tensed for the slightest sound. But only a lifeless silence drifted under the door.

Perhaps he had simply imagined it, the rose on the sill, the words on the wall. Perhaps there was nothing there at all, nothing but his imagination. And if he went through that door again now, what he discovered there this time might be utterly different.

He reached into his shirt and took out the book. On the far side of the room the blanket nailed to the window billowed slightly. As he stared at it now he

182

seemed to see a figure in the folds, the slack g.
face drooping forward, light spilling from the holes
that were its eyes. He could see a mouth now, or
that shadowed hollow that imagination made a
mouth. It seemed to be smiling. If he looked long
enough he knew the thing would tear loose from the
window and fly down.

He forced his eyes away and willed his feet to
move toward the door. When he was midway across
the room the charred refuse that littered the floor
flickered briefly and was gone. Where the odor of
dampness and cinders had been there was now the
smell of cigarette smoke in the air.

He bumped into something. Something sharp and
light grazed his forehead and bounced away. He kept
his eyes riveted to the ground, knowing full well that
if he glanced up now he would find the spike-jawed
squadron of Spitfires back in place, tethered to the
ceiling on weblike strands of wire.

Behind him now he heard the light, sinister gurgle
of the aquarium filter starting up. Everywhere there
was the sudden and overwhelming presence of Scott.

He could picture him sitting there majestically on
the edge of the bed, smiling over at him, smoke
pluming through the air about him in pale blue
tendrils. And he wanted with all his being just to
turn around and find things the way they had been
four months ago when it had all started. Yet he
knew now, with a certainty past all speech, that if
he did turn, whatever was waiting there would
destroy him.

He reached out and wrapped his hand around the
handle of the door. Just above the drone of the filter
he heard a voice. Scott's voice.

"Well, well. Look who's here."

It wasn't real, he told himself. It was only an

183

seemed to see a figure in the folds, the slack grey face drooping forward, light spilling from the holes that were its eyes. He could see a mouth now, or that shadowed hollow that imagination made a mouth. It seemed to be smiling. If he looked long enough he knew the thing would tear loose from the window and fly down.

He forced his eyes away and willed his feet to move toward the door. When he was midway across the room the charred refuse that littered the floor flickered briefly and was gone. Where the odor of dampness and cinders had been there was now the smell of cigarette smoke in the air.

He bumped into something. Something sharp and light grazed his forehead and bounced away. He kept his eyes riveted to the ground, knowing full well that if he glanced up now he would find the spike-jawed squadron of Spitfires back in place, tethered to the ceiling on weblike strands of wire.

Behind him now he heard the light, sinister gurgle of the aquarium filter starting up. Everywhere there was the sudden and overwhelming presence of Scott.

He could picture him sitting there majestically on the edge of the bed, smiling over at him, smoke pluming through the air about him in pale blue tendrils. And he wanted with all his being just to turn around and find things the way they had been four months ago when it had all started. Yet he knew now, with a certainty past all speech, that if he did turn, whatever was waiting there would destroy him.

He reached out and wrapped his hand around the handle of the door. Just above the drone of the filter he heard a voice. Scott's voice.

"Well, well. Look who's here."

It wasn't real, he told himself. It was only an

echo, the shell of something that had happened here once, trapped in the ravaged walls and released now.

"You're not going to believe this, Craig, but I was just thinking about you today."

Yet it *was* Scott's voice. Mildly mocking, and at the same time infinitely seductive.

The book in his hand seemed to move. He forced himself to loosen his grip, to let it go. For an instant it appeared to hang suspended in the air, and then it fluttered to the floor and fell to pieces.

He could hear someone walking outside on the breezeway. He hesitated, then slowly turned the handle and opened the door.

The glare of the sun was momentarily blinding, but as his eyes fell into focus he saw a small diapered figure standing there staring at him, thumb tucked securely in his mouth, index finger softly massaging his nose.

They locked eyes, and in that instant he stepped free of the room, drawing the door closed behind him.

"Birdie," cried the little boy, pointing a plump hand at the roof as the pigeons took to the air in a startled flurry.

For a second he thought he heard his name being called, the dull slap of a palm against the door.

And then it was gone, and there was just he and the little boy, standing together on the breezeway, following the flight of the birds.